COOKIES AND SCREAM

CEECEE JAMES

For my Family

CONTENTS

BLURB

Tour guide Georgie Tanner has always encouraged her clients to enjoy the realism of an American Revolutionary War reenactment - but today things got a little too real. When one of the actors doesn't get back up after the battle, the crowd is horrified to find out he's really been shot. Patrick Armstrong, local high school teacher, is dead.

Georgie's old high school friend, Terry Brooks, is arrested for the murder. A man with a young wife and a baby, he seems the least unlikely suspect. But, with hundreds of people as witnesses, there's no denying he was the one who pulled the trigger.

He begs Georgie for help, and she's determined to do her best. After all, he'd never do something like that, would he?

Her sleuthing skills slowly uncover other possible suspects, but, try as she might, she can't shake the sight of the smoking gun gripped in Terry's hand. And then she uncovers something that terrifies her. Suddenly, Georgie is afraid that what she might have just sealed the case against her old friend.

This book is a work of fiction and although it does discuss events and places from the American Revolutionary War, the setting of the book is a fictional town utilizing facts from the war in order to enhance the story.

CHAPTER 1

Old Bella, as I fondly—and sometimes not so fondly—called my refurbished catering van, was a very reliable mode of transportation, faithfully carting the Baker Street Bed and Breakfast guests participating in my historical tours from one momentous site to another.

She could also be a stubborn old cuss.

Like now, for instance. I'd been trying to start the van for five minutes, but thus far, she'd only whined each time I turned the key. I pumped the gas, my seat pulled all the way forward so I could reach the pedals—short girl problems—and gave the customers a reassuring grin in my rearview mirror.

Come on, come on. You can do it. You can do it, baby.

The guests glanced at one another with a little concern, and I could tell they were wondering just what they'd gotten themselves into.

Boom! With a backfire and a giant plume of smoke, she finally fired up. I nearly kissed the steering wheel in gratitude.

"We're fine! Everyone buckled up?" I yelled over the rattling of the engine.

On the bench seat behind me, a retired married couple checked to make sure their seatbelts were extra secure. Another man buckled his on, trying to act nonchalant.

A rattling and shaking van that starts like a gunshot will do that to a person.

Today, my guests included three businessmen and the older couple. All five people were staying at the B&B, owned and run by my Aunt Cecelia.

Well, she wasn't really my aunt, but being best friends with my grandma, she'd long ago earned that title. And, now that my family was all gone, Cecelia was all I had left.

This morning, I was about to take the guests on a historical tour offered by the bed and breakfast. Charles, one of the businessmen, a dark-haired man in his mid-forties, almost hadn't made it for the tour. He'd gone to look for a good cup of coffee, as he called it, and had only just made it back in time to climb into the van.

"Where's your coffee?" I asked Charles when I noticed his hands were empty. "Did you drink it already?"

"Couldn't find a descent stand in this little town," he growled. A deep, disappointed sigh eased out of him.

"Don't worry. I know a good one," I reassured him. As the guide, I was more than happy to drive tourists all around our little town of Gainesville, a place rich in American Revolution history. I really enjoyed taking visitors to ancient sites, like graveyards, buildings, and museums. And, even though I'd only been at the job for just a little over a year, I'd grown up around here, so I also knew where to find the best cup of coffee.

Most of the bed and breakfast's clientele was a combination of history buffs and retirees. But during the summer, the B&B saw quite a few young people hoping to spot a ghost in one of the touted haunted houses on the tour.

Almost all of the guests I'd had so far had been fun. Retirees' were some of my favorite tourists. They always had a ton of questions, and sometimes, they had stories to share as well. It might take a good forty minutes for the story to come out, but I didn't mind. It seemed the quiet ones always had the best stories, shared with distant looks of nostalgia.

It was funny, but over the last few months, I'd become known as an "expert" of local history. I kind of prided myself in that.

It's strange how quickly life can change. Just over a year ago, I was working nearly sixty hours a week commuting to Pittsburgh as a paralegal to a lawyer who specialized in estates. A lot of the families in that area had war memorabilia passed down through the generation, and part of my job had been figuring out the worth of those heirlooms.

I'd been engaged to my long-time boyfriend, Derek Summers. But one nightmarish moment changed all of that, when I'd witnessed his car swerve off the road without even hitting the brakes. The explanation I'd been given was suicide, but I just couldn't believe that was true. And so, with Derek gone, I'd moved back home.

I'd felt like half a person for a while there, almost as if I was living in a gray world. Everything had lost its color for me. But, slowly, through months of Cecelia's patience and some good counseling, I was finding myself again.

This morning, I couldn't help the butterflies of excitement, my first in a long while. Today was a special day for our little town, one that came around only once a year.

I tucked my short dirty-blonde hair behind my ear—a new haircut and I was still getting used to it—and spun around in my seat. As best as I could, I raised my voice to make sure everyone could hear me. "Welcome aboard Baker Street B&B's Historic Tours! You guys are lucky to be here this week because today, we will be visiting Apricot Creek, the site of one of George Washington's last battles. Every year, they do a reenactment of that battle, and people come from all over Pennsylvania, and even farther, to participate. It's actually been televised once for the History Channel. So please get comfortable. I'll fill you in on some fun tidbits about the town as we make our way to Apricot Creek."

From the very back, Charles gave me a thumbs-up, and I was reminded to go look for some coffee. The two other businessmen, Doug and Stew, nodded in my direction. The retired couple, the Laceys, gave each other pleased smiles.

"Okay, folks. Let's take a ride back in time." Corny, I know, but I still loved to say it. I shifted again, and Old Bella lurched forward.

As we rattled down the dirt driveway and out onto the road, I began my spiel. "Apricot Creek is a little-known battle site from 1794. Led by George Washington during one of his seven trips into Pennsylvania, twelve thousand soldiers came to this area to stop the Whiskey Rebellion."

"What caused the rebellion?" Mrs. Lacey asked. She reminded me of my Grandma, with her cute smile and curly white hair. She wore glasses and held hands with her husband.

I sighed happily. I wanted a love like that.

"Glad you asked," I said. "I was just getting to that part. The rebellion began when Alexander Hamilton, then the secretary of state, proposed a tax in 1771 on alcohol. The tax was intended to help the United States out of the huge debt it had incurred during the American Revolution. Well, the American public was outraged, and by 1779, the rebellion threatened the stability of the newly formed United States. President Washington tried for several years to come to a peaceable resolution, but the violence escalated. Finally, he put on his old general's uniform and led his soldiers to squash the rebellion, making him the first and the last president to lead the troops. Apricot Creek is where one of the resulting battles took place. Eventually, the militia apprehended one hundred and fifty people and tried them for treason."

I hit my blinker and pulled into the drive-through of a coffee stand. As we waited in line, I glanced in my large rearview mirror at my guests, like a school bus driver. "Who'd like a coffee? Tea?"

The businessmen were surprisingly simple with their order of three Americanos. The retired couple declined, with Mrs. Lacey joking about a hummingbird-sized bladder. Her husband nodded pretty vigorously at her words, so it was probably a good thing she skipped it. As for me, my budget was a little tight this week, so I opted out, as well.

Ten minutes later, with the coffees in hand, we were back on our way. As I drove them through Gainesville, I pointed out the local small-town eateries, antique shops, and a few of the older landmark buildings. Little bits and pieces of my childhood spun around in my mind as I shared with my passengers. No matter how many times I led this tour, I always felt a wave of sappiness for my hometown.

For instance, this ice-cream shop right here. Sweet Treats, it was called. I remembered my grandma and grandpa taking me here every Sunday after church. They'd give me a dollar and I'd stare at all the flavors, eventually settling on the one I got every time—green pistachio. Grandma always told me that's why my eyes were green, because I ate so much of it growing up.

And over there was the five-and-dime store that always had its display window filled with antique trinkets. I'd purchased my first "historical find" there, a rusty coin. I was ten, and was convinced it was from the Revolutionary War. About a week after that, my bratty friend (and Cecelia's grandson) Frank pointed out that the coin was just an ordinary token from an arcade.

I drove out of Gainesville and toward the Apricot Creek historical park, continuing with my history lesson. "During the Whiskey Rebellion, eight American soldiers broke off from George Washington's battalion for a scouting mission. Led by Colonel Berkshire, they ran across rebels during the mission. The rebels were well armed, and it could have been a disaster."

I continued to describe how George Washington and the rest of the soldiers arrived in the nick of time to triumph over the rebellion. "They used bayonet-tipped muskets and drove the rebels back from the hidden scouts. Shots were fired, but surprisingly, few soldiers were injured. This ushered in the first real peace to the new United States."

The road we were on skirted the edge of the mountains. Mountains around here were different than the ones found out west. Low and rounded and beaten down by time, they were gorgeous in autumn with colorful foliage. But now, as we headed into winter, they were brown with the bare-leaved trees, sprinkled with evergreens.

I pulled the van through the Apricot Creek park entrance and into the parking area. Large Beech trees hemmed the border of the park. People could be seen meandering about the large grassy area in the center. Most huddled in jackets and wore knitted hats to protect against the cold temperature. But others appeared as if they'd stepped right out a history book.

I parked the van, and slowly, we all got out.

"I'm excited for this," Charles said with a grin. He zipped up his jacket, while the other two businessmen nodded.

Doug pulled a blue beanie from his pocket, and put it on his head before blowing on his hands. At least, I hoped it was Doug. Both he and Stew looked so similar, from their short, brown hair, to their loafers and khaki pants, that it was hard for me to tell them apart. I'd taken to just smiling and trying not to get into a situation where I had to address them by name.

"What was it you do again?" Doug asked Charles.

"I'm one of the curators at the New York City Museum of American History," Charles said. I could see the pride in the twinkle in his eye.

"That's really amazing," I said. "I have a feeling this is going to be a real treat for you."

"Definitely." He gave the field an appraising look. "You never know. Maybe we can create an advertising partnership between your town and our museum."

My eyebrows rose with excitement, and I gazed out at the actors preparing for the simulated battle. *Do your best, guys! This could really be something amazing for our little town.*

Charles nodded in my direction as the three businessmen broke off from our group and headed toward the open area.

"Where do we go to watch?" Mr. Lacey asked me, his arm around his wife's waist. The retired couple were adorable.

They were both were short in stature, and wore identical plaid scarves over their coats. Mrs. Lacey had on a white hat with a giant pom-pom. They were what I'd call professional travelers. The two of them had already been all around the world, and had previously shared their experiences with me about different cruise ships and tours. I couldn't help feeling a tiny bit of pressure wanting to make this a good trip for them.

I grabbed my knitted gloves from my pocket and put them on. "Well, if you want to follow me, there's actually some bleachers set up right over here."

There was the sound of a shot fired.

Mrs. Lacey blanched. "Good grief. Are you sure this is safe?"

"Yes," I hurried to reassure her. "It's perfectly safe. They're just shooting blanks with replica 18th-century rifles. Sometimes, I think it's their favorite part of the simulated battle." I grinned. "There's never a shortage of volunteers to play the soldiers."

"Look, Henry." Mrs. Lacey smiled as she pointed. "Do you see that man right there? He looks like George Washington!"

I tried to follow where her finger was pointing. The actor really did resemble George, but I knew he was actually portraying Colonel Berkshire, leader of this historical battle. The tall, lanky actor was our local high school's history teacher, Patrick Armstrong. He was fairly new to our school, and I hadn't heard too many good things about him. His biggest sin was that he'd failed our star quarterback, causing the teen to be ineligible to participate in the state play-offs a few weeks back. I was a little surprised the teacher was brave enough to show his face around town at all, since the high school team lost that game.

Patrick now had his arm outstretched, pointing in one direction as he instructed the placements. He'd taken over as the ring leader of the reenactment for the last two years.

He'd done a good job, and the yearly reenactment had garnered even more attention. Last year, the National Historical Society had honored him, along with the rest of the reenactment group, on their web site.

Unfortunately, Patrick wasn't just a stickler for historical accuracy. He had a mean streak, as Cecelia would say.

And, from all the rumors I'd heard, I'd be hard-pressed to find someone who'd argue with her about that.

CHAPTER 2

I led the Laceys along the path toward the temporarily erected bleachers.

"Is it always this cool this time of year?" Mrs. Lacey asked. Her cheeks and nose were red.

"Anything in the low fifties is actually pretty mild for us. But the weather is known to change fairly quickly. The wind can act up, and when it does, it usually brings snow."

"Oh, brr," she said, dramatically cuddling herself with her arms. "I'll be grateful, then."

Mr. Lacey helped Mrs. Lacey up a few rows. They settled into a remaining space in the already filling seats. My three businessmen had already chosen to sit in the first row.

I usually liked to sit on the top tier. That one gave the best view of the many action scenes. But, instead of taking a seat, I stood to the side and people-watched the growing crowd.

There was the familiar hustle and bustle of the local high school students. The history class had a long tradition of offering extra credit for those who volunteered for the reenactment. Patrick had kept up that tradition.

There was also a gathering of community college thespians who walked around griping in frustration at the teenagers who kept shooting blanks at one another. They made up the other half of the soldiers. The military leaders were almost always played by history buffs in their thirties and older.

I cracked up as I caught one uniformed man pull out his cell phone. A Colonial-dressed woman scolded him. His cheeks turned red as he slid it back into his hidden pocket.

But overall, the scene was impeccable. There were a few chickens scratching in the grass by one of the houses. A woman worked an old-fashioned water pump. Several children ran about wearing dresses and short pants.

Even though I'd watched it many times through the years growing up, I couldn't help but be impressed. Except for a few oops like the phone, it really was like stepping directly back into a different time.

I glanced over at the tourists to see if they were enjoying the scene so far. Mr. and Mrs. Lacey seemed into it, both of them pointing at various things as they talked to one another.

The businessmen all had their phones out. I sighed. I guess you can't please everyone.

"Georgie!" a voice called from my left. It was my old high school friend, Kari Missler.

We'd originally been friends in the barest of terms. She'd been the head cheerleader, while the only thing I led was the championship of most books checked out at the library.

But a funny thing happened after graduation. Now, I'd pretty much always been me. But those who'd pinned their entire identity on their high school popularity were suddenly at a loss and had to go through a crash course of "Who am I?" that most of us had been doing the entire four years.

Anyway, Kari was someone who'd clung to me that summer. I'd brought her into my little group of friends and shown her my favorite swimming holes, and she taught me some makeup tips. When I moved to Pittsburg and she went away to college, we still remained in contact.

But she loved the boys, and it was no surprise to me when she dropped out just a few months shy of her graduation to get married to a great guy named Joe. Eleven months later, she had her first baby. Less than a year after that came baby number two.

Through the years, we'd always talked and texted. Last year, she was the second person I told that Derek had been killed. Now we both were living back in the same town. It was a relief to have a friend to confide in.

Tucked under the knitted hat, her hair was still the same bleached blonde from high school. She was thin, but not as thin as she always complained she wanted to be. Still, her face always held a happy smile. And darn it all if she wasn't still just as peppy.

"Georgie! I've been looking everywhere for you! You're late." She bounced over to me wearing a sky-blue ski jacket.

I smiled and met her half-way. "Sorry. I had to stop for coffee."

"So...." She glanced around. "Where are they?"

"Who?"

"Your group. The people you bring here."

I made a shh face. "There's no way I'm pointing them out to you. You'll just stare at them, and then they'll know we're talking about them," I said, shaking my head.

"Any good-looking ones?" As usual, she had on a full face of makeup, including false eyelashes. She winked, and I marveled they didn't fly off like a pair of butterfly wings.

"Kari!" I laughed. She may be happily married, but like I said, she'd always been about the boys.

"What? I'm just asking. I can look, can't I?"

"It's a retired couple and a few businessmen."

"Businessmen?" Her gaze flicked to the bleachers, and the interest drained out of her voice. "Oh, boy. It's not those stiffs in the front row, is it?"

I nodded without even looking. Trust her to pick them out.

She wrinkled her nose. "Not impressed. They look about as fun as a warm bowl of jello."

Another laugh erupted out of me even though I'd been trying not to react. Even worse, she'd said it in her "quiet voice," which was quiet enough to get heads to turn in our direction.

"Kari, shhhhh!" I grabbed her arm and dragged her away from the stands. "Where's your husband? Kids?"

"Joe's around here somewhere. Christina and Colby are out causing trouble. Probably dismantling the guns as we speak."

I immediately glanced at the wood-hewn table by the buildings. It was covered in muskets laid out for the actors to pick up.

She caught my glance and snorted. "Please. Do you think you

could catch those kids? They're sneaky and fast, God love them."

I smiled again. I knew she was kidding.

I hoped she was kidding.

"So anyway, I wanted to tell you," Kari continued. "Did you hear what happened here earlier?"

"What happened?"

"Girl, that's what happens when you're always late! We had a real fight on our hands. No reenactment. I truly thought it was going to come to blows."

"Are you serious?" My eyebrows rose. "Tell me!"

"Well, you know who...." Her index finger ran along her bottom lip and then shot out to point to Patrick. I observed him for a moment. He was dressed in period clothing, with a tricorn hat on his head, yelling directions at one of the kids pushing the wheelbarrow. Was his voice scratchy? He did seem more flustered than usual.

"Dane Evans came over and yelled at him." Her eyes narrowed as she continued to stare at the history teacher.

While she did, I glanced over at Dane, the quarterback's father. He was a bald, husky man with mean, deep-set eyes.

I zipped my jacket up a little higher. "I can understand, but

Armstrong said he failed him because the teen had too many absences. Rules are rules. The coach had no choice but to bench him."

"Well, you've heard the rumors about the last school Armstrong was at." She arched an eyebrow conspiratorially, quiet voice in full force. Her lips pursed, and she tapped the bottom one with her index finger, appearing deep in thought.

I knew what she was getting at. I'd heard the rumors. "You're talking about the dirt that he charged the football players for a passing grade at his last school?"

"He did charge them. I'm convinced of it." She crossed her arms. "But that school was a Double A, and winning in its district. I think people were too scared to have that taken away from them. There was an investigation, but nothing came of it."

I could understand why. If it was true, it would mean that the school's wins would be forfeit. I could see the school letting the teacher go instead.

"Oh, Colby! Over here!" Kari yelled and waved her arm. "I'll be back later," she said over her shoulder, and then dashed across the grass field.

I looked for her nine-year-old son. She'd been right after all. He was looking at the muskets, tongue sticking out, eyes wide with excitement. As I watched, he touched a bayonet.

Thankfully, she reached him just in time and scooted him to the side. He started to protest loudly, but Kari marched him along with a smile on her face. They disappeared behind one of the buildings.

Before I could see where they went, a male voice shouted over the crowd. It was Jared Inglewood, the high school gym teacher. His role was not just as an actor, but also as the reenactment narrator.

"Ladies and gentlemen. If everyone could take your seats! The battle is about to begin. We ask that the audience remain seated until the show is over. Do not come out or approach any of the actors. You may see blood. You may hear groans. Trust me, it's fake. Feel the thrills, the fear, and the courage. Root for the side of your choice. But most of all, please enjoy the show."

I walked back to the bleachers and climbed up the rafters. There was limited seating, but I finally found a place near the top.

Men hurried into their formation lines, with a few picking up their muskets from the table on their way. Soldiers in uniforms faced off against farmers and townspeople.

The gym teacher gave a short monologue, outlining the battle and events that led to it.

Patrick took his place in the center of his line of men. His arm went up. The saber in his hand glinted in the sun that had just peeked out from the clouds. With a swoosh, it came down and he screamed, "Charge!" His breath clouded white in the cold air.

Both sides lunged forward before stopping approximately ten yards from one another. The long-barreled muskets came up and were held horizontal to the ground. Then there was a multitude of explosions as the firelocks ignited the black powder.

The scent of burning gunpowder filled the air. Several men fell to the ground with screams and moans, while others began to quickly reload their weapons.

Around me, the audience reacted with cheers and applause. Some of them coughed at the billowing smoke.

More musket blasts filled the air. I frowned as two men—or teenagers, I couldn't tell—stood as if frozen, staring down at the prone body of Patrick. I was surprised to see the teacher on the ground. I hadn't seen him fall.

As if the two soldier's stares were contagious, the musket fire slowly ceased around the history teacher. The militia quit fighting back. It seemed as if the US army was falling apart.

One of the soldier's dropped to his knees at Patrick's head. "Stop! Stop!" he screamed.

The audience shifted uncomfortably. Was this supposed to happen?

Another soldier joined the first. He fanned the teacher's face.

Now, the farmers and townspeople raced forward, seemingly more bloodthirsty than ever. But as they ran across the empty lawn, more men dropped to the ground by Mr. Armstrong's side. It only took another second for the running combatants to realize something was very wrong.

Their leader called for everyone to stop. Suddenly, this wasn't a game any longer.

The audience all around me began murmuring. I heard snippets of, "What's going on?" and "Is this supposed to happen?"

It was broken by a clear shout from the leader of the farmers and townspeople. He'd reached Patrick and started to unbutton the history teacher's uniform. "Everyone back! He needs air. We need an ambulance! He's been shot!"

The crowd sat frozen for only a moment before they poured down the bleachers. The metal steps clanged and vibrated all around me with the footfalls. Hearing that live ammunition had been used caused a panic. People bolted, screaming, to the parking lot. A few brave people ran out to the field.

I watched all of this for a second before I climbed down

myself. I walked out to the scene, clutching my cell phone. I was about to call 911 until I saw several people talking on their phones.

The voices around the teacher quieted down to murmurs. I couldn't tell what was going on. Between the legs of one of the soldiers standing over the teacher, I saw Patrick's eyes, open and vacant, staring into the sky. A small red trail of blood tinged his lips. My hands flew to my mouth as I realized Patrick Armstrong was dead.

CHAPTER 3

*T*he next hour was a blur of ambulance personnel and police. After the initial investigation, the paramedics placed Mr. Armstrong on the gurney and covered his face with a sheet. I gathered my tour group around me and tried to shield them from the sight.

"When can we go home?" Charles asked. His face was grim and his hands were jammed into his coat pockets.

"I-I'm not sure," I said. "It looks like the police are still questioning everyone."

A firm hand clamped on my shoulder. I turned to see Frank, Cecelia's grandson, and my old classmate.

And antagonizer. He'd been such a nuisance throughout our school years, famous for tattling on me, calling me Georgie

Porgie, and pulling on my pigtails. Things changed in high school, where we mostly ignored each other.

I'd been forced to reconnect with him when I accepted the tour job from Cecelia. He'd just returned to Gainesville himself, having served in the military until an explosion landed him in the hospital. Now, he was a part of the town's police force.

Things had actually been going pretty well between us. I'll be the first to admit I was surprised. He was still grouchy, but I'd almost seen him smile a few times now. I kind of took it as a challenge. And it didn't hurt that he'd somehow grown into his six-foot-plus height, changing from a string-bean to well-muscled.

We took a few steps away from the tourists to talk.

"Surprise, surprise. Fancy finding you here," he said dryly, his hand rubbing his dark hair. He replaced his police hat. "Right smack in the center of trouble, like always."

"Did you forget? It's what your grandma pays me for, to run these tours."

His mouth snapped shut. He stared out at the field, his blue eyes narrowing. "You see anything?"

I shook my head. "No. I didn't even see Patrick go down. But, earlier, I did hear something kind of suspicious."

He pulled a toothpick from his pocket and stuck it in his mouth. "What?"

I started to tell him about Dane Evans, the football player's dad, when Mrs. Lacey tugged on my elbow. She had the hood of her jacket up, covering her white hat. Worry wrinkles lined her forehead and mouth.

"Georgie, this is so upsetting. Can you find out if we can go back to the B&B? Is there someone you can ask?" She looked pointedly at Frank.

I glanced at Frank, and he nodded. "Go ahead. Take them home and then come back here," he said. "I want to finish this conversation."

"All right, everyone," I said, waving my hands to gather in the other four tourists. "Officer Wagner says we can leave now. I'm so sorry this happened."

There wasn't any discussion as we walked through the parking lot. Everyone was solemn as they boarded Old Bella. I clipped my seatbelt and adjusted the mirror to look at the tourists.

"That was horribly upsetting. Are you all doing okay?" I asked.

The five of them gave various replies of affirmation that they were all right.

The three businessmen actually didn't seem that bothered. In fact, they started talking about it right away. I swore I saw more than one grin flash across each of their faces as they discussed the death.

Poor Mrs. Lacey though. Her face was as pale as milk. Her husband patted her knee and whispered encouragement in her ear. She gave a stiff nod, her eyes sad and wide.

"So, what does everyone want to do?" I asked. "You feel like going to another place to explore, or would you like me to bring you back to the B&B?"

"I want to go back," Mrs. Lacey blurted out. "I can't even think of doing anything else. Some poor man was shot right before our eyes."

"You can bring me back too," Doug added. The other two businessmen nodded in agreement. "I've got my car. I might just do some exploring on my own." I heard him discuss with Charles and Stew if they wanted to join him.

"Okay, then," I said, fixing my mirror. "Everyone buckle up."

The parking lot was a zoo. As I crawled, bumper to bumper, for the exit, I had to force myself not to replay the memory of what I'd just seen.

Patrick Armstrong was definitely dead, and based on

everything going on lately, I was quite sure it wasn't an accident.

Behind me, I could hear the businessmen laughing. Their laughter ripped through me like fingernails on a chalkboard.

The drive home seem to take forever. Finally, I pulled into the bed and breakfast's driveway. Cecelia was outside, decked in a winter jacket and a pair of gloves, with pruners in one hand. Her white hair was covered in a red, knitted cap, complete with a matching scarf. She watched us curiously as I parked, obviously realizing we were back early.

Slowly, everyone disembarked from the van.

Cecelia walked toward us. "Oh, dear. Long faces. Something must have happened." Her gaze attached to me, and her eyebrows lifted in question.

Mr. Lacey led his wife into the house, his hand comfortingly on her back. Two of the businessmen headed for one of their cars. Charles stood in the background as if waiting for me.

My heart heavy, I filled Cecelia in with what had happened at the reenactment.

"No!" Her hand flew to her mouth. She shook her head in disbelief, but, like the trooper she was, she rallied quickly. With a glance to the house, she outlined her plan of action. "Well, I'll go in there and see about those two. I'm sure the poor things are in shock. Some homemade cookies and hot cocoa might just do the trick." She took off her gloves and dusted her hands on her pants as she addressed Charles. "Mr. Vanderstill, will you be joining us?"

Charles shook his head. "No, I'm going exploring with the other two. I just wanted to talk with Georgie for a moment, when you've finished."

"Okay, then." Cecelia gave him a nod and walked into the house. I had no doubt that the Laceys were in good hands.

"How can I help you?" I asked Charles. He was much taller than my five-foot-two, and I had to look up.

He pressed his lips together as if unsure of how to start. "I noticed something today. I'm not sure how good this information is, but I figured I should probably let someone know."

"Okay." I smiled encouragingly.

"Well, something struck me as odd about one of the muskets. The bayonet seemed brighter on one, with a newer patina to the metal. And the musket stock appeared to be made of a different grain of wood. As I looked, I thought maybe the trigger guard was different, too. Just something I noticed. As a museum curator, these things stand out to me."

"Wow. Okay, thank you. I'll let them know."

His gaze turned bashful. "Uh, did you know him?"

I shook my head. "Not well."

"But it was still a shock, I'm sure."

"Very." I tucked my hair behind my ear.

"Well, I'm sorry. You did a great job taking care of us." He smiled, and his hazel eyes sparkled. "All right. Just wanted to be sure to get that detail out. Now, I guess I'm off." He stepped backward, jerking his thumb at the others waiting in the car. "Who knows what kind of trouble they want to get into."

"You guys should check out the Boar's Head Tavern while you're out and about. They have great draft beer."

"Sounds good. You have a good day."

I watched him walk away, smiling a little. Charles Vanderstill. Hmm. He wasn't bad looking. Not bad at all.

I thought about the musket as I waved, watching the car head down the driveway in a cloud of dust. Something else I needed to tell Frank. With a sigh, I climbed back into my van and followed the trail of dirt, turning left at the end of the driveway to head back to Apricot Creek park.

CHAPTER 4

*B*y the time I returned to Apricot Creek, parked the van, and walked out into the field, over thirty minutes had passed since I'd originally left. My stomach felt like a lead ball as I spotted crime scene tape marking off the area where Patrick had died. Both soldiers and townspeople sat intermingled, talking together on the bleachers. Standing near them were a few officers.

I glanced over at the town setting. The muskets had been lined up, with little white tags hanging off each bayonet. Probably to denote who had been using which one.

Another pair of officers were with a boy over by the reenactment armory tent. I recognized him as Colby, Kari Missler's young son. Her husband, Joe, was standing behind the boy, his hands clapped on his son's shoulders.

Where was Kari?

I turned in a circle to search for her. Ah! There she was! Talking animatedly with another officer, her daughter clinging to her hand. I walked over, zipping my jacket as I went. It was cold and getting colder by the minute. The ground was oddly squishy under my feet. It gave me the shivers as I passed by the yellow caution tape.

Kari glanced up as I approached. Her eyes appeared tired and stressed. "Georgie! I've been looking everywhere for you."

The police officer nodded to acknowledge me. He was short, just a little taller than me, but burly like a bull dog.

"I'm sorry," I said. "I had to get the guests back to the B&B. Is everything okay?" I jerked my thumb in Colby's direction.

Kari nodded. "Someone saw him when he was touching those the rifles on the table. The police are asking him a few questions. Joe's with him."

"They'll be done with the boy in just a minute," the officer said. "I'm Detective Preston. You witnessed the shooting?" The question was aimed at me.

I shook my head. "Mr. Armstrong was already down on the ground before I even noticed. But one of my guests saw something of interest. That's actually one of the reasons why I came back here."

The detective tipped his head, obviously curious at what I had to say. "Yes?"

"So, one of my tourists is a curator at the New York City Museum of American History. He seems pretty knowledgeable about muskets. He wanted me to know that one of the muskets had a few differences that made it stand out from the rest of them. A different trigger guard, patina, and wood stock. Can I see if I can point it out to you?"

Detective Preston glanced at the muskets before give me a measured stare. "What was your name again?"

"Georgie Tanner." I swallowed nervously.

He nodded. "Let's go take a look. But don't touch anything."

Kari came with us as we walked over to the muskets. Like I'd assumed earlier, the flags were marking each one with a name.

I could easily see what Charles meant as I got closer. It was obvious enough that the police probably didn't need my help. One of the muskets was conclusively a cheap replica. But the thing that might not be as easily noticed was that it was a flintlock, not a firelock. I could easily identify that from my experiences as an estate paralegal. It differed from the muskets the actors used in the reenactment which used burning hemp to light the gunpowder. But this cheaper one was flint-based.

"You see this one here? It's a flintlock." I pointed to the musket.

There were two teenagers standing nearby. Neither looked comfortable.

"Hey," I addressed them. They both jumped, and one flushed from the attention. "Are you guys part of the group that sets the muskets out on the table?"

"Yeah," the more gangly one answered.

"You hand them out to the actors?" Detective Preston asked.

The teen's eyes looked like they were about to bulge out of his head, he was so nervous. He swallowed. "Yes, sir."

Detective Preston read the tag on the flintlock. "Can you confirm that this one was given to Terry Brooks?"

I flinched at the name and glanced at Kari. We both knew Terry. We'd gone to high school together. Now he was back teaching intermediate math at the high school.

The kid swayed. I honestly thought he might pass out. His friend answered for him. "Yes, sir."

"Did you notice it was different than the others?"

"The other volunteer said it was special. Said that Mr. Armstrong told him to give it to the guy who'd be shooting at him. I told him that was Mr. Brooks."

"Was it loaded prior to being on the table?"

"Mr. Armstrong always packs the paper charges for the other weapons. I didn't think this one was any different. When Mr. Brooks came to get his weapon, he didn't ask. He just grabbed it and went to his place."

The first teen frowned. "That's not how I heard it. That volunteer guy told me it was Mr. Brooks, not Mr. Armstrong, who brought the weapon here. That it was super important to Mr. Brooks that only he use it."

"Where's the volunteer that you're talking about?" The detective gave them a steely glare.

They both craned their necks to look around. Both came to the same conclusion: "I don't see him."

"What was he wearing?" the detective asked. "What did he look like?"

"Just a hoody and jeans." The braver one shrugged. "He had the hoody pulled up with sunglasses on."

The gangly one swallowed again. "The hoody had a banjo on the back of it. I saw him talking with Mr. Brooks later."

Detective Preston sighed. "Where's Mr. Brooks now?"

The boys pointed to a teacher sitting on the bench with the

other actors. Terry Brooks looked stressed, his head in his hands. My stomach was in knots.

"He was the one leading the charge of the townspeople?" the detective asked.

The teens nodded like bobble heads.

"Did Brooks say anything when you gave him this? Did he look at it like it was out of the ordinary?"

The gangly teen's face flushed in a mottled pattern.

"Well?" Detective Preston prodded.

"He said, 'I finally get to do what I've been looking forward to for a long, long time.'"

"And did he tell you what that was?"

The teen wobbled some more.

His friend nudged his arm. "Chill out. This isn't your fault."

The first teenager nodded. "He said he was going to kill that scumbag, but we just thought he was getting into character."

Kari cleared her throat, drawing the attention her way. "I may have some light I can shine on that subject. It's pretty well known that he and Patrick Armstrong have a bit of a legal dispute going on. They're neighbors, and it has to do with a tree on their property lines. Rumor at the PTA has it that

35

Patrick countersued for over two-hundred thousand and it looks like he may win the court case. Something about the preservation of trees over a certain age...." She shrugged and twisted a wisp of her blonde hair.

The detective narrowed his eyes at her words. "And Brooks didn't do anything else suspicious? Just grabbed the different musket and went on his way?" he asked the teen.

"No, nothing else weird," the gangly one answered. "He took the musket and left."

Detective Preston thanked them for their help. He put on some gloves and picked up the musket. Without another glance at me, he walked over to the officers questioning Colby. I followed after him.

When he reached the young boy, he squatted down on his haunches. His grumpy face was arranged in a weak simulation of joviality. "So, I heard you were looking at the rifles earlier, huh?"

Colby nodded. His face showed he wasn't fooled by Preston's attitude. The kids looked serious and afraid. I felt bad for him. I'd never seen the kid without a smile before.

"You're not in trouble," Detective Preston reassured him. "Now, was there something that stood out to you to make you want to look at the weapons?"

Colby nodded again. His tongue dabbed his bottom lip.

"What was it?" the detective asked.

The boy looked up at his father. Joe squeezed his shoulder. "Go on, son. Tell him what it was."

"I heard that man over there." Colby pointed to Terry Brooks. "He said he couldn't wait to get his hands on his musket, because it was special. I wanted to go see what it was."

Detective Preston nodded and slowly rose to his feet. His leathers creaked. "Anything else?" he asked the officers standing there. Although he was shorter than them, I couldn't tell by the bravado he had.

"The kid's story just corroborated the other stories we've been hearing," one of the police officers said.

"All right, then. I'm going to suggest you go ahead and read Mr. Brooks his rights. Bring him down to the station so we can interview him. Get someone to wrap up this weapon and photograph all the other muskets. I need everyone who touched this musket to be fingerprinted."

Even though I'd heard everything, I still was shocked as I watched one of the officers radio the officer standing by the bleachers. It felt like a nightmare as the police approach Terry. Terry's eyes flew open when he realized what was happening. He started to shout. Roughly, the officer turned him around and cuffed him.

I spun back to the detective, but he was already walking off, talking into his phone. Colby leaned against his dad, biting his bottom lip.

I hurried back to the two teenagers still standing by the tent. "The other volunteer? Tell me what he looked like again?"

The boys looked just as clueless as before. "Just some guy in a hoody," the gangly one said. "I don't remember anything particular about him, other than he seemed to be Mr. Brook's friend."

"And you're positive you don't see him now?" I asked.

They gave a half-hearted glance before the second boy shook his head.

"Keep looking. I'll give you twenty bucks if you find him," I said, about to walk away.

The first teen said, "Wait. What about that one guy? Bald."

"Oh, yeah." His friend nodded enthusiastically. "Yeah, that's right. Ben's dad. Ben's the quarterback at our school."

"I know who he is. You're saying the dad was over here?" I asked again.

"Yeah. He was looking at the muskets, too. He picked one up with a big grin."

"Yeah, that's right," the braver teen agreed.

"Hey, do we get the twenty bucks?" the first asked hopefully.

"You keep looking for that volunteer who brought the gun. I'll give you fifty now, if you can point him out to me."

Shouts from the bleachers grabbed our attention.

"I have a baby and a wife! I would never do something like this!" Terry yelled. He glanced in my direction and recognized me. "Georgie! Please help me!"

My heart squeezed as his voice brought back a memory of him crying out for me in that same way in high school. I'd seen a bunch of kids gathering behind the gym, and went back there to check it out. Terry Brooks was in the center of the group, being pushed around. At the time, I'd jumped right in to help him without a second thought.

Well, I didn't know exactly what was going on now, but I guessed I was about to do it again.

CHAPTER 5

"Hey!" I yelled to Detective Preston. He ignored me as he directed the rest of the officers in different ways.

"Detective Preston!" I yelled again, jogging across the lawn.

He turned around, his eyes wary. I ran up, trying not to act like I was breathless. I really needed to get some more cardio in.

"Yes?" His tone was clipped, expressing impatience.

"There's one more person you could talk with. Those teenagers said someone else was by the muskets. The quarterback's dad."

"A dad," he deadpanned. I couldn't tell, but it sure sounded sarcastic to me.

"Yes. They'd been fighting and—"

He interrupted, and this time there was no mistaking his placating attitude. "Thank you very much, Ms...."

"Tanner."

"Ms. Tanner. I'd love for you to go down to the station and give a statement. Include your story of seeing a dad by the muskets."

"It wasn't me," I said, lamely. "It was the teens over there. They said..."

He cut me off with an impatient look. "Like I said, share your version of the events down at the station. Now, if you'll excuse me."

He rapidly walked over to one of the police cars.

Wow. That detective just managed to not only hit my pride, but stomp all over it. I hated being dismissed like that. I took a deep breath. Terry wanted my help, and I needed a clear head to be able to do it.

Okay, to the police station it was.

The drive there was a blur as I kept picturing Detective Preston's face and me punching it. I'm not so sure I was all that cooled down by the time I got to the precinct. Old Bella was too big for the tight-angled parking in front of the building, so I had to drive the van around to park it in the back. As I pulled the keys from the ignition, I took a few more breaths to calm myself again. Between my anger, and the memory of Patrick's death, I was afraid to even close my eyes for a second, not wanting a flashback of the poor man's eyes staring at nothing. I grabbed my purse and climbed out.

Immediately, the wind slicked my hair back. I ducked my head and pulled up my hood. The wind got worse as I rounded the building, pushing me back with every step. Finally, I was able to get inside.

"Can I help you?" The clerk spoke without looking at me, typing furiously on a keyboard.

"Yes," I gasped like I'd just gotten off the elliptical. "I was supposed to come down and make a statement about what I saw at the reenactment scene."

"Oh, yes." She pointed down the hallway. "Go on back to the left. There should be an officer waiting at his desk."

I followed her directions. It reminded me of the first time I'd been here, at seventeen after a prank had gone bad at the high school. There were rows of chairs in the booking room to my right. Several men sat there looking bored. One man was up against the wall getting his picture taken. To my left were two large windows. One was dark, and the other lit. As I passed, I peeked inside and saw Terry sitting in the room at a table, his head in his hands. An officer was sitting across from him.

Oh, boy. This was just all too real. I swallowed and continued to the back room. I wrinkled my nose. The scent of stale coffee was so strong it could have been coming from a room deodorizer. There were four desks spread out in the medium-sized room, each one covered with a mountain of paperwork. Jefferson, one of the officers I was previously familiar with, sat at the far desk.

He looked up as I approached and flicked a finger toward a seat across from him. It seemed my presence made him notice the mess on his desk, as he started to clear a space. After shoveling a pile into one of the desk drawers, he pulled a pad of paper and a pen out from another. I swallowed as I lowered myself into the chair.

"Georgie." He briefly smiled to welcome me. "So, you were there this morning?"

I nodded. My fingers found a loose thread on my jacket and started to twist it.

He silently read from the paper and then looked up. "You were able to identify the musket that was used in the murder?"

The use of the word murder sent a flash of ice through my

veins. Obviously it was murder. But knowing I'd witnessed it, was an actual bystander as a poor man got cut down right before me, brought tears to my eyes. I nodded again, and tried to swallow the lump in my throat.

"Can you describe for me what the difference was between the muskets that helped you identify it?"

Hesitantly, I told him about the two types of rifles and their different firing methods.

He took careful notes. "And there's no way to confuse it, correct? You know the trigger is firing differently with a flintlock?" he clarified. The paper was covered in scribbles.

Again, I nodded. My skin felt clammy. Terry had asked me for help, and so far, all I was doing was giving the police more ammunition to use against him.

"Did you hear about the lawsuit that he was involved in with Patrick Armstrong? And the counter-suit in the amount of two hundred and fifty thousand dollars?"

Again, a sick nod.

"Did you hear him speak out against Patrick Armstrong, or threaten him in any way?"

Here, I shook my head. "I've known Terry since high school. He's always been a nice guy. I just can't believe he'd kill someone like this. Not unless it was to protect his family."

That got his attention. "So you think he would kill someone if his family were threatened?"

I shifted uncomfortably in my chair. It felt harder than ever. "Well, sure. Wouldn't most people?"

He didn't respond to my question, writing even faster. "There's one more thing. We also discovered Mr. Armstrong's car had been broken into at the event. Did you see anything you might deem suspicious at the parking lot?"

I shook my head. "No. Nothing."

He wrote down some more and then pushed the paper over for me to sign. After I finished, he took the pen back. "Thank you for coming down, Georgie. I'll let you know if we need anything else."

Feeling dismissed, I walked back out into the hallway. Standing outside one of the interrogation rooms were two officers, each holding a Styrofoam cup of coffee. They were quietly talking and staring through the window.

"Poor sucker. He's in for the long haul," one said and took a sip.

"Look at him. He doesn't even realize how guilty he sounds."

"Excuse me," I interrupted, walking up.

Both officers turned toward me, each wearing different expressions of suspicion.

"Can I help you?" the one with dark hair asked.

"Is there any way—any way at all—that I could talk to him? Just for one minute? I just have one question. I'm sort of an antique expert. It was me who pointed out the weapon used." *Bluff. Bluff. Bluff.*

The dark-haired officer laughed. "You've got to be kidding me. Sure, just go on in and chat up our number one suspect."

The second one with short blond hair paused, his eyes narrowing.

The first looked at him. "You can't really be considering what she asked. Come on, Daniels. That's ridiculous. Wait until Sheriff Parker hears about this."

"Hey," said the one called Daniels. "Chill out. The Sheriff likes some of my unorthodox ways of getting information. We might actually learn something." His gaze flicked back to me. "Thirty seconds. That's it. The door stays open, and you stay in the doorway. One false move, and you'll be joining him in a cell. We'll be here watching." His tone lowered with the last sentence, and I knew he was trying to scare me.

Well, it worked.

The blond officer opened the door and I walked in.

Immediately, I locked eyes with Terry, hoping to telegraph that he needed to act like he didn't know who I was. I was strictly trying to pose as an antique expert.

"Hello there. My name's Georgie. I just want to go over some procedure issues about the use of an unauthorized musket in the reenactment."

His eyes had widened with recognition, and his mouth dropped. But when he heard the serious tone in my voice, it seemed to clue him in. He frowned briefly before his face relaxed and he nodded.

"Sure," he answered.

"Why were you using a different musket than everyone else?" I asked. That was my biggest question.

"Mine was missing and it was the only one left in the rack. I knew Patrick wanted us to stay on schedule and figured he brought it as a backup."

I pressed my luck and asked a second question. "Did you know those rounds were live?"

"Are you kidding me? No!" His eyes nearly bulged as he slapped the table.

I winced at his reaction, feeling Daniels tense next to me. I tried a more soothing tone. "Okay. Is it part of the procedure to check?"

"No." His head dropped into his hands. "I should have, but Patrick was such a stickler. It didn't even cross my mind that there would be live ammunition on the set. Especially since it was stressed to me that he'd brought the musket."

I nodded, trying to play it cool. I licked my bottom lip, already knowing I'd pressed my luck by asking more than one question. But there was one more I was dying to ask him.

"Who was the guy in the hoody?'

"Hoody?" he asked, looking confused. "I don't know what you're talking about."

I nodded, not wanting to trip Terry up into saying something that might incriminate himself.

"Thank you for your answers." I started to back away.

"Hey, hang on a second. Georgie? You have to tell them I didn't do it. I have a baby! Maybe it was an accident? Maybe Patrick stocked the wrong charges for it? I don't know. There are a lot of people besides me angry at him right now."

"Okay, time to go." The dark-haired officer stepped in and grabbed my arm. "You've asked your questions, so you can head out now."

I left the interrogation room feeling more confused than ever.

Years ago, my friend had been bullied as a teenager. From

everything I was hearing, it seemed like Mr. Armstrong was bullying him through the lawsuit now. Had Terry possibly come up with a crazy plan to get his revenge? One that he could carry out himself, in full view of an entire audience?

I felt around in my purse for my phone, preparing to call Kari for more info about the lawsuit as soon as I got outside. As I headed toward the exit, a woman was entering the station. Her blonde curly hair blew around her as she came through the door.

"Where is he?" she screamed.

CHAPTER 6

"*M*a'am?" The front desk clerk rose to intercept the crazed woman. The woman's blue eyes were out of focus as she stumbled toward the desk. Both the clerk and Daniels ran to the woman's side to stop her, the officer reaching her first.

"Just hang on there," he said, firmly gripping her elbow. "Who are you looking for?"

"Let go of me!" she yelled back, her face red from emotion. She tried to jerk away, but the cop wasn't letting go. "Where's Terry? Where's my husband?"

The way that Daniels was looking at her, she'd soon be finding out. By joining him in the next cell. I needed to calm her down.

"Hey," I said, soothingly. "It's okay. Take a deep breath. Everything's going to work out."

"Everything is not okay!" she yelled, her hair flipping in front of her face. "It never will be again."

"Okay, but I'm here to help," I said, moving closer. I felt like I was walking up to a feral cat.

She tried to jerk her arm away again, giving a low growl.

I watched nervously as Daniels' partner's hand strayed close to his cuffs on his belt.

"Calm down," I said, sharper this time. "Think of your baby!"

That seemed to get to her. She quit struggling, but still stared wildly through her mane of hair.

"Ma'am, I'm going to need you to quit resisting," Daniels said. Then he asked me, "Who is this again?"

"What's your name?" I asked.

She looked desperately at me, mascara running down her face. Her gaze flicked up to the cop holding her arm before it met mine again. "Emily," she whispered. "Emily Brooks."

"Okay, Emily. We'll figure this out."

"I can't believe they took him," she whimpered. Emily stared up again at Daniels. "You're hurting me."

"You going to calm down? I'll release you if you stay calm." At her nod, he slowly let go of her, like she was a dog that might be rabid.

She rubbed her arm. "Can I see him? Please?"

The second officer answered her. "Your husband? We need to finish processing him, but—"

"There's no harm in—" Daniels said at the same time.

"Again, Daniels?" The second cop rolled his eyes.

"Look," Daniels said, "we'll give you a second to tell him you love him. But after this, you need to get him a lawyer. If you can't afford one, the court will appoint one."

"Oh, we have a lawyer all right." She huffed and crossed her arms. "Fat lot of good he's done us."

Daniels glanced at his partner. "Just go get him and have him stand by the room's doorway." And then to Emily. "You stay right here, got it?"

She nodded again, her eyes searching fearfully down the hallway.

The dark-haired cop grumbled some more, but went to get the prisoner. I heard some clanging and the door opened. A minute later, he stood with Terry outside the interrogation room.

Emily's face collapsed into tears at the sight of her husband. "What happened?" she cried. "Why would you do this to us?"

"Emily!" Terry's voice was sharp. "I didn't do anything. I'm going to be okay. They'll see it was an accident."

"You threatened him, though—"

"Stop it now, Emily. I love you. Now go take care of Luke." Terry addressed the officer at his side. "I'm ready for this visit to be over."

The dark-haired cop looked at Daniels, who gave him the thumbs-up, and Terry was taken back into the interrogation room.

Officer Daniels escorted Emily to the front desk. I made my escape as he was going over the protocol with her, as well as the possibility of a bond.

I headed to the van, unsure of what to do next or where to even go. It had crossed my mind that I should probably not involve myself anymore, but the look on Terry's face in the interrogation room pulled on my heartstrings.

Like I said, I'd seen that look of fear and helplessness on his face before. In school, he was the typical geeky one that the jocks and bigger boys liked to pick on. They pushed him around, throwing his books, and dumping his bag. And then one day, it went too far.

I remembered hearing the muffled shouts from behind the gym building. I knew before I saw anything that it was Terry and the typical horde of goons. I ran around the corner and saw broken glasses on the ground and Terry's resigned face, bleeding from the lip. A meaty fist came from above to land another blow. Without thinking, I slid my backpack down from my shoulder, heavy with my math and history books, and gripped the strap. With a grunt, I swung, catching the brute on the back of his big head and sending him sprawling against the wall.

The fight ended with laughter as the bullies teased the wrestler who'd just been beaten by a girl. I didn't wait around, but snatched up Terry's glasses and reached my hand out to help him up. Together, we ran back into the building, only stopping when we reached the library entrance.

"Thank you, Georgie." He'd been embarrassed as he put his glasses back on and smoothed down his hair.

"Don't worry about it. I've got your back."

Surprisingly, that defense was enough to cause the bullies to leave Terry alone. And a friendship had been forged between us that day. Nerds unite!

Now, once again, I'd seen that fear and helplessness etched across his face, and my brain demanded I still be that friend.

I unlocked Old Bella and climbed in. Before starting it up, I pulled my phone from my purse to call Kari.

She answered on the second ring. "Georgie! You disappeared again! Where are you now?"

"At the police department."

"Police! Good grief! Girl, you get around."

"I had a tip about someone else who possibly handled the muskets, so they wanted a statement from me. How are you guys? How's Colby? That poor kid's probably scarred for life."

"He's doing okay. It was a good life lesson for him to learn not to touch things that don't belong to him. Honestly, I can't believe this insane day we've all had. Did you see Terry down there?"

"I did. And his wife showed up just as I was leaving. Poor thing was a mess."

"Oh, Emily." She sighed. "Her baby is just six months old. Probably still dealing with hormones on top of this nightmare."

"Well, she didn't do him any favors, that's for sure. She

announced to the whole department that he basically threatened to kill Armstrong."

Kari groaned. "Well, I can't say that I blame her."

"What's actually going on with this lawsuit? You were saying that Armstrong had counter-sued for over two hundred thousand. And you think that he might win?"

"Yep. Honestly, have you ever heard of anything so ridiculous? Patrick said he was asking for damages for pain and suffering, as well as the bad rap his reputation was taking being labeled, as he called it, 'a monster.'"

"What was this originally all about?"

"I don't know everything, but Jenna, the head of the PTA, told me that the entire fight is over a massive black walnut tree that's on Armstrong's property. The tree is extremely rare, extremely old, and extremely unsafe. Sometime last year, the tree got struck by lighting. Somehow, it's still alive, but split, with the side closest to the Brooks' house leaning in their direction. If that arm collapses, it will land right on their house. I heard the room nearest to the tree was the baby's. Those two have been fighting about it this entire time, with the Brooks wanting the tree cut down, and Armstrong saying he must preserve a national treasure. And now with the possibility of losing the lawsuit, plus over two hundred thousand, and still having his family in danger, well...I could see how that would push anyone over the edge."

"So, you think Terry did it?" I asked, my voice low. I almost didn't want to hear what she had to say.

"Georgie, Terry was never very strong. But a rifle and rage gives a person the muscle that sometimes the constitution lacks. I can't say he's innocent. Especially when it comes to threatening his loved ones."

I groaned, remembering I'd said almost that exact thing to Officer Jefferson.

After making plans to get together for lunch later in the week, we hung up.

Drumming my fingers on the steering wheel, I considered my next step. It only seemed logical to go check out this famous tree.

Little did I know what I was really going to find.

CHAPTER 7

*I*t seemed ridiculous that someone would kill another person over a tree, but then again, I had seen more than a few crime shows that proved anything was possible. Still, it just didn't seem like Terry was that type.

But, as for his wife, I couldn't be as sure.

The benefit of being a tour guide was knowing the entirety of the town like the back of my hand. It didn't take me long to find the two teachers' homes, and see the massive black walnut tree between them.

I parked the van across the street and studied the tree and two houses. The trunk was definitely rooted on the history teacher's side. As impressive as it was, it was obvious the tree was old, even dying. Leaves lay in rotting piles against its base. Black marked the trunk where lightening had struck, splitting the tree into a V. One arm of the V hung precariously close to the Brooks' small farmhouse. If the baby's room was on that side, it truly was a disaster waiting to happen.

The refusal to cut it down seemed to be strictly malicious. As much as I understood preserving history, it made no sense why there was even a chance that the court case could be ruled in Patrick's favor.

I shook my head in disbelief and got out of the van. The breeze was cold and bit my cheeks and nose. I reached into the back seat and pulled out my jacket. With it zipped and the hood pulled up, I stuffed my hands into its pockets and ventured across the street.

Maybe it was just my imagination, but up close, the tree even smelled ancient and mulchy. The bark had crumbled at the V, making a sawdust pile at its base. I stared up into its bare boughs. The branches curved with a heavy majesty only seen in a tree of this age and size. As dangerous as it appeared, it was also easy to see why it was so loved.

I walked around the tree, my hand briefly leaving my pocket to touch the rough bark. Something on the ground caught my attention.

It was the corner of what appeared to be a white envelope

poking out from a pile of rotten leaves. Curious, I bent down to brush back the leaves. The envelope appeared to be pinned down by a rock. Rain had caused the typed words on the front to blur, but I could still make them out.

Patrick Armstrong.

I carefully picked up the envelope and turned it over. The envelope flap was open, whether by human hand or moisture, I didn't know.

Had it flown off of Patrick's front door or porch? Or had it intentionally been left here at the base of the tree? I hesitated a moment. *You know better. Don't do it....*

Ignoring that inner voice, I pulled out the folded paper from inside.

The words were typed and softened from the rain. But I could still read it.

I tried to reason with you. Are you seriously going to let this ruin his life? That scholarship guaranteed him four years at university! You'll regret failing him. You wanna ruin my son's life? Let's see how you like it.

Wow. I remembered Kari talking about how upset Dane Evans, the quarterback's dad, had been at the reenactment. This had to be from him. Without a doubt, both he and his son were obvious suspects.

But what if this note had been planted by someone who was trying to set up that football player? This whole situation was just that crazy. The more I looked, the more suspects came popping out of the woodwork.

Crazy or not, the important thing was that the note gave Terry's case reasonable doubt.

Slowly, I stood up, my imagination playing out my return to the police station with more evidence. I was going to get myself put on the suspect list, if I wasn't careful.

The visual made me nervous and I got out my phone to call Frank. I figured he owed me, since I'd taken out the garbage and dragged the cans to the street, after our "family" dinner last week, even though Cecelia had asked him to do it. Pretty lame reason to say he owed me, I'll admit, but it was enough for me to feel okay about ringing him up.

"Wagner here," he answered, his voice gruff as usual.

"Hey, Mr. Cheerful," I said, needling him a bit. "Any chance you could swing by the Armstrong house?"

There was a pause. Either he was trying to figure out a comeback, or he was wondering what I was doing at a murdered victim's house.

"Go on," he said. Curiosity must have won out.

"So, I found this envelope with Armstrong's name on the front."

"Weird," he said dryly. "Was his address on it, too?"

"It was hand delivered," I replied. "No address. But what was inside is what matters."

"You opened it? That's a federal offense, genius."

"It didn't come through the post office. No stamp. Are you listening or what? It had a typed-written threat..." I paused, looking up at the house. Had I just heard something?

"Keep going," he said. "Don't stop now when it's just getting good."

There it was again.

"Shhh," I hissed, ducking behind the tree trunk. It was definitely coming from inside the house. Who could be in there? Patrick Armstrong lived alone, as far as I knew.

"Georgie?" Gone was the teasing tone. His voice was sharp and serious. "What's going on?"

Another bang happened, and then the sound of glass breaking. My gaze bounced over the windows and door, trying to figure out where the sound was coming from.

"Frank, someone's in the house," I whispered. "Or they're trying to break in right now."

"Get back in your van and lock the doors. Move!"

I glanced at my van, but suddenly it seemed very far away, and very much out in the open. I felt safer hiding behind the tree.

"I've got to go," I whispered.

"You aren't going anywhere!" he shouted in return.

"Keep it down!" I hissed again. My skin felt prickly with nerves as I hazarded another glance around the tree. "I have to call 911."

"And just who do you think you're talking to right now?" he snapped back. "I'm already on my way."

I'd have felt stupid at his words if my heart wasn't already pounding like a base drum at a rock concert. "Well, hurry up then." I peeked again. This time, my jaw dropped. A man rounded the corner.

"Frank! I see him! I see him!" I scrambled through my purse for a can of pepper spray.

The man turned toward me, and I gasped. I knew exactly who he was.

CHAPTER 8

"Stop right where you are, Jared Inglewood!" I yelled, springing out from behind the tree. I held the pepper spray in front of me. "I'm already on the phone with the police."

Jared Inglewood, the high school gym teacher. Seriously? Were all the high school teachers turning into criminals today?

I held the pepper spray with a steady hand, and had my sternest face on. When he'd first seen me, shock flashed across his face. But now it held a mixture of desperation and anger.

"Look, I wasn't doing anything," he said, his hands held up before him doing a "calm down" motion.

"Georgie! Stay away from him," came Frank's voice through the phone.

Jared's muscles tensed. I had no idea what he was about to do, so I tried a friendlier approach. "What's going on, Jared? Why are you here?"

His legs trembled and I honestly thought he was about to race away.

I faked my friendliest smile. "Hey, I didn't mean to startle you, I just saw you come out the window... I'm sure you have a reasonable excuse." *Hurry up, Frank!*

He shook his head, still staring at me.

"I have pepper spray and the police are on the way."

Immediately, he began to stumble backward.

"Jared Inglewood, seriously, if you run, you'll only make it worse for yourself."

My reasoning must have gotten to him. The tension left his body. He sank back down to the ground and put his head in his hands. He pulled them away and looked at them, dazed. Blood covered his palms.

I reached into my purse for a wad of tissues and handed them to him. "Why are you bleeding?"

He wiped the tissues across his face. "What have I gotten myself into?" he mumbled.

"Tell me what's going on."

"I can't believe this is happening. Everyone's going to find out."

"Find out what?" I asked, continuing to try and sound friendly.

"I... I have a debt. Just a small one. I swear I was going to pay it back!"

"Okay. I believe you. How'd you get the debt?"

"I had a sure thing at the horse track. The jockey, he pulled it at the last second..."

"A gambling debt? What's that got to do with Patrick Armstrong?"

Sirens could be heard in the distance.

"I had to borrow the money from the gym program. It was just for the weekend. I was going to pay it back on Monday!" Jared's eyes desperately sought mine. "Patrick found out somehow. Said he had proof and was going to destroy my career. That has to be illegal, right? To threaten someone like that?"

He groaned as the sirens grew louder. "I didn't want him

dead. Honest, I didn't. I just wanted to see what proof he had." His head flopped back into his hands. "My life is ruined."

I wanted to ask more, but two police cars pulled up then. Frank slammed the door of his and marched over like a muscle-bound Mac truck. Exiting the other car was Jefferson.

"You couldn't handle this on you own?" I asked Frank out of the corner of my mouth.

"I erred on the side of caution. I didn't know if I'd need backup."

"Hands up!" Jefferson yelled.

I stepped back as Jared raised his hands in the air. Jefferson snapped the cuffs onto Jared's hands and pulled him to his feet.

Jared winced as he stood, his hands still bleeding. "I'm sorry. I didn't take anything." He stared back at the house.

"But you broke into a murdered man's home?" Frank raised an eyebrow. When Jared didn't answer, Jefferson took the teacher to the back of his police car.

I watched Jared go, agreeing with his assessment that he was a stupid man. Why would he risk his family, job, and even freedom? I wondered what kind of proof Patrick had—if it was pictures, letters, or what.

"What were you doing here anyway?" Frank asked me. Jefferson returned and stood listening.

"I was trying to see what the tree fuss was all about. The one involved in the lawsuit that everyone says was Terry Brooks' motive."

Both Jefferson and Frank glanced over at the black walnut tree.

Then I remembered the note. "Oh, and I forgot. This is really why I called you." I held it up.

"I'm glad to see you carrying that." Frank pointed to the pepper spray in my other hand as Jefferson took the envelope. "But it's for emergency situations only. You can't really rely on it to protect you."

"I'm just glad I had you on the phone."

"Hmm, maybe I am good for something." His eyes twinkled humorously at me. Great. Now I'd never hear the end of how he came to save the day.

I cleared my throat as Jefferson bagged the envelope. "Um. I did happen to see the letter. It seems like a pretty clear threat made to Armstrong by a student's dad. You know, the high school quarterback that couldn't play in the state finals? Lost his chance for a scholarship?"

I looked between them, expecting a reaction. It seemed like an obvious motive to me.

They didn't give me one. Instead, Jefferson walked over to the house and put crime scene tape over the window. I heard him on his mic calling for a relative to be notified.

"Where did you find the note?" Frank asked.

I led him to the tree and pointed at the base. "Right there."

He slipped on a pair of gloves and squatted down. Carefully, he rifled through the leaves. With a raised eyebrow, he lifted the rock.

"Under this?" he asked.

I nodded.

"So, there's a reasonable chance that this was left for Mr. Armstrong and he never saw it."

"I thought of that. I also thought maybe it had blown along with the leaves and ended up there."

He stood with a deep exhale. "How about you get back to doing your tour thing, and leave the police stuff to us?"

I bit my lip, feeling foolish. Had I ruined a clue? "Sorry. I saw it and reacted. I didn't think I needed to call the police for spotting a piece of paper."

He looked disappointed, which made me feel worse. Discouragement descended on my shoulders like an x-ray apron. Since when did running a historical tour make me think I was able to investigate a modern murder in my small town, anyway?

CHAPTER 9

I drove back to Cecelia's, feeling like I either needed a hug or a bed to pull the covers over my head.

When I got there, I noticed that the car the group of businessmen had taken off in earlier still wasn't back. I was glad they'd found a way to salvage the day. I started for the porch, musing. What was it they said they did again? I remembered one saying he was into pharmaceutical sales, and the other was the museum curator. I couldn't remember what the third one had said....

A little white puff ball hurtled toward me.

"Bear!" I squatted to call the neighbor's Pomeranian to my arms.

That crazy dog didn't come. Instead, she chose to run hyper circles around me. I dove this way, and the animal dodged to the left. I went left, and she jumped to the right, all the while with her tongue hanging out in a happy dog grin.

"Bear! I'm not playing. Come here."

At those words, the dog took off running for the opposite end of the driveway, all pell-mell, her curly tail wagging.

Fine. Desperate times called for desperate measures. "Peanut!" I hollered. "Come here, sweetie! Peanut!"

The fuzzy puff skidded to a stop at the sound of the new name. Oscar, the neighbor, had inherited the dog when his wife passed. He'd tried in vain to call her Bear, spurning Peanut, as "too sissy."

The little dog, however, had other ideas.

"Come on, girl," I cajoled, my fingers out. I made a few kissy noises. "Come on, Peanut."

After a moment, the dog raced back to me, ears back, tongue hanging out, clearly pleased with herself. She jumped into my arms and proceeded to cover my cheeks in doggy kisses. I struggled to keep my mouth safe, which she took as a challenge, making that the new target for her tongue.

"Come on, you stinker. I just took you for a walk yesterday," I whispered into her soft fur as I carried her across the lawn and down the neighbor's driveway.

"Hold your horses! I'm coming!" Oscar O'Neil yelled out in response to my knock on his front door.

I knew it could take a while for the crotchety old man to make it to the door. He wouldn't admit it, but he suffered from arthritis. Which was one of the reasons why I'd volunteered to walk Peanut a few times a week.

When I'd first met him, he was the definition of a recluse. I couldn't say much had changed since we'd become...I wasn't sure if friends was the right word. But he let me walk his dog and bring him some food. And there was one weekend where I helped clean his porch from the months of stacked unread newspapers and other garbage.

His house was still in sad disrepair, I thought, as I glanced at the peeling paint. I'd have to tackle that job in the spring, when it was warmer.

He finally opened the door. Today, he wore a green sweatshirt that sported a Christmas tree, and blue plaid pajama pants. Old slippers clad his feet. His face was covered in white whiskers, his nose was red and his eyes bleary.

He blinked at me. "Did that darn dog escape again?"

I hugged Peanut. "Here she is. And, I'm sorry, but she's still not responding to Bear. You might want to..."

"She'll do it. She just needs to adjust." He reached for the dog and I handed her over. He cuddled her for a second under his chin. "You're just stubborn like your mama was, aren't you?" He gave her a kiss, and then jerked back when he realized I was still standing there. "Well? What do you want?"

That man. If he wasn't grouchy, he'd have no personality at all. "Are you sick? You feeling okay?"

He wrinkled his nose. "Well, aren't you lovely? Come over here and tell me I look sick." He coughed into his hand. "Just a touch of the croup. I'm fine." He turned to go.

"Want me to bring over some chicken soup?"

That got his attention. He glanced back. His puffy brows lowered over his eyes suspiciously. "You'd do that for me?"

I nodded. I didn't know why he was always so surprised when I offered him anything. "Sure. Just give me a few minutes, and I'll bring some right over."

"Carol used to make that." He stared at the ground, and darn if his eyes didn't look a little misty. He wiped at his nose. "Dog hair getting in my face. I'll see you in a little bit." With that, he shut the door behind him.

The sun was starting to slip down the horizon as I meandered down the driveway, giving off that cooler light that made the shadows stretch like they were trying to run away. I walked up the B&B porch and went inside.

The first thing I saw was the Laceys seated in the formal living room. Cecelia was with them and they were playing cards. The scent of freshly made cookies filled the air.

"GiGi!" Cecelia's soft voice welcomed me from her spot on the couch. Her white hair was pinned up in its customary bun. Her use of my old nickname made me smile. "How are you doing, darling? Come and sit with us for a while."

"Hi, everyone. What are you playing?" I perched on the arm of the chair and glanced at the coffee table. The surface was covered with cards, along with three mugs of hot cocoa, each partially finished to different degrees.

"Hello, Georgie. We're having a rousing game of hearts," Mrs. Lacey said. "Would you like to join us? We've just nearly started."

"No, no. You guys go ahead. I'm going to grab something to eat, if that's okay?" I glanced at Cecelia.

Cecelia's cheeks rose with her smile like two red balls. "Of course it is. Go eat! Shoo!"

I rose and waved goodbye, before heading into the kitchen. It was here the fresh cookie scent blasted me, along with the warmth of the stove. Cooling racks had been laid out on nearly every surface, each rack filled with soft cookies.

Breathing in deeply, I walked over to inspect them. She'd made quite a few flavors. Chocolate chip, butterscotch, white chocolate chunk with macadamia nut. Chocolate oozed out from the buttery cookie.

I'd really gotten into cooking shows after one long night in front of the TV when I couldn't sleep—and thought about that one episode when the chef had talked about using applesauce instead of eggs.

I took a crumb—because everyone knows crumbs don't have calories—and popped it into my mouth. Mmm. I'd never known how to bake, and only recently had the interest to learn. Especially since it would almost be a shame to waste an opportunity to learn under a creator of old recipes like Cecelia.

Turning from the cookies, I got out a pan and put it on the stove. After a quick search in the freezer, I found Cecelia's stockpile of chicken soup. I clunked the frozen cube from the baggy into the pot and turned it on low.

The scent of the cookies was overwhelming. I picked up a chocolate chip and poured myself a glass of milk. I grabbed a pad of paper by the phone and cleared a space for myself at the table.

Now, what have I gotten myself into?

I started a list.

One History Teacher murdered.

Enemy one: his neighbor was losing a legal dispute with said teacher. And coincidentally also fired the rifle which killed Mr. Armstrong.

Enemy two: Jared Inglewood, who was caught breaking into the Armstrong house to retrieve evidence he was being extorted with.

Enemy three: Dane, the quarterback's dad who yelled at the teacher at the reenactment. Possibly left a letter on the Armstrong's property.

One unknown person who was said to have meddled with the muskets. But the witness was possibly unreliable.

I bit my lip as I read over the list. Think...Georgie. The answer's here somewhere.

After a few minutes staring until I felt bug-eyed, I pushed the paper away. The answer might be there somewhere, but I sure wasn't seeing it.

Maybe I needed to get back to my apartment. Cecelia seemed to have everything under control here. I'd check back in with her later.

I stirred the soup and poured it into a bowl. After set the bowl on a plate, I arranged a row of saltines along one side, and a few cookies along the other.

Just before I walked out, I snagged two more cookies for myself. After all, they were made with whole wheat and eggs. I knew that was on the food chart somewhere.

"You okay if I go home?" I stopped outside the parlor to ask Cecelia. "I can come by later."

"Are you not feeling well?" she asked, her eyebrows raised in concern at what was in my hands.

I glanced at the soup. "No, this is for Oscar. He's kind of under the weather."

"Oh, poor man. You go ahead and go home. I've got everything handled tonight."

I thanked her and told the Laceys that I'd see them in the morning, then headed to the neighbor's.

He was slightly less cranky when he came to the door this time, only asking, "What's this?" in regards to the cookies.

"It's a pile of broccoli," I said, lifting an eyebrow. "It's good for you."

His mouth trembled in an almost smile. I held my breath, but he didn't let it break forth. "Smart aleck," he muttered, taking it from me and closing the door again.

Hopefully the cookies would sweeten his disposition. I got into my van and headed home.

I had to admit, I did start to feel more relaxed when my apartment building came into view. It wasn't fancy, but the building was close enough to downtown that I never felt like I missed any action. Which was a big deal, after moving here from the city. I punched in the code to open the front door and waited for it to buzz. When it did, I wrenched the heavy door open and walked inside.

The owners of the property had done their best to preserve the old-world charm of the building. Walnut ceiling trim gleamed from a recent polishing. The stairs were dark wood, with a lovely curving banister. The foyer and stairwell glowed from antique wall sconces that had been refitted to current electrical standards.

I headed up to my place on the fourth floor, possibly the only downside to this apartment. At least it was some exercise, I always reasoned, as I walked down the hallway to my door. Although that excuse didn't work after doing a weeks worth of grocery shopping. As I rounded onto the landing, I heard the neighbor's TV going off with a game show. The spicy scent of sausage permeated the air. Mrs. Costello was probably making spaghetti, a meal she sometimes brought over to share if she knew I was home.

I opened my door. Frank had installed a new lock a couple months back. It was super sticky, and the key hard to turn. But he insisted it was safer than the weak one I'd had before.

I headed for the lamp. Once again, I'd forgotten to leave a light on when I left that morning. It was getting darker now as we approached winter, and although it wasn't quite nighttime, it was dark enough in my apartment for me to have a difficult time seeing.

I threw my keys down on the table with a grimace. The table was covered in painting supplies, with my newest canvas propped up on the easel. I'd started a complimentary one to my river scene, this one focusing on a rope swing we had set up around the river's bend. Summer of my youth, it called to me. The painting was about two-thirds done, but I wasn't motivated to finish it now. The couch was tempting me. I kicked off my shoes and headed over. It was about time for my favorite baking show, and hey, I still had cookies to eat.

Just as I was about to sit, my cell phone rang. With a groan, I dragged myself back to get it from my purse.

Of course, it was buried at the bottom, with each ring stressing me out as I dug for it. "Hello?" I finally answered.

"Georgie? It's me, Emily Brooks."

Terry's wife. "Oh. Hello, Emily." I carried the phone to the couch and sat. "What's going on?" I could hear a baby crying in the background.

"I'm sorry." She was sniffling. My eyebrows went up when I realized she was crying, too. "There's something I have to tell you."

CHAPTER 10

"What's going on, Emily? Are you both okay? Do you need to get the baby?" I could feel the tension ratchet in my gut at the crying in the background.

"Just a minute," she said. I heard murmuring, and then the baby quieted. "Okay, I'm nursing him."

Her voice was soft and seemed so much younger than someone in their mid-twenties.

"Why did you call?" I asked. "Is it Terry?"

"Yes." She sniffled. "Terry said that you were a safe person. I don't know what to do. We can't afford the bail. I'm scared, Georgie. I'm afraid he did it. Just point blank shot him. He's been so stressed out lately."

My spine stiffened. I wasn't sure why she called me, but I knew I didn't want to hear that. "Emily, I'm here for you. But don't tell me anything that might incriminate Terry. Save that for your lawyer. Were you able to find one yet?"

She gave a sarcastic huff. "We have one. He's been useless in the tree case."

Her mentioning the tree made me think of the letter. "Have you seen anyone over there? By the tree or even knocking on Patrick's door? Any strange cars? Visitors?"

Emily murmured to her baby, and sounds of patting could be heard through the phone. I figured she was burping him. "Well, there was one person," she said slowly.

Immediately I seized it. "Who? Can you describe him?"

"Medium height. Well dressed. Fancy haircut."

My stomach fell. That definitely did not describe Dane Evans, the balding quarterback's father. That could have been anyone, even Patrick's lawyer visiting.

"Thank you for trying to remember. As far as Terry goes, emotions are high right now. You have the right to be completely freaked out. Just don't assume anything. We're going to figure this out."

"My entire life is falling apart." She broke down in tears.

"I know, Emily. It's rough. Do you have any family living nearby? Maybe your mom?"

She took a shuddering breath. "Y-yes."

"Why don't you go there for a few days? Give your whole house, the tree, everything a break."

She seemed to think that was a good idea, and by the end of the conversation, she said she was going to pack. Knowing she was leaving for her mom's made me relieved. I wouldn't have to think of her rattling around in that house feeling lost, her baby crying. She'd be getting support while the lawyers figured this out.

Please, oh, please. Let the lawyers figure it out.

———

THE NEXT MORNING, I rolled over in bed with a groan. My entire body hurt like I'd hiked up a mountain. It was amazing what stress could do to a person.

It had taken me forever to fall asleep once I went to bed. Terry's face, the letter, Dane Evans, the furious quarterback's dad, Jared Inglewood—all those thoughts rolled around in my mind. Once upon a time, I could only sleep with the help of prescription medicine. It had taken a while, and a counselor's support to finally wean off. But on the nights I tossed and turned, I still missed it.

The guests were scheduled to leave the Baker Street Bed and Breakfast this morning, so Cecelia had texted that I needn't come in early. Check-out day meant a different job for me: flipping the B&B and getting it ready for the next incoming guests.

Hot coffee brought me somewhat back to life. I stood by my window, sipping, and stared out into the street. My mind was still wandering over Patrick, but a car trying to angle into a tight space caught my attention. Along here, cars were always parked bumper to bumper, and it was trying to get into the last open spot.

I understood the difficulty. When I'd first moved here, I'd hated parallel parking. But I was getting pretty good at it now.

The gal pulled in and drove back out a few times. By the third time, I was really feeling bad for her. Fourth time, fifth time.... *Surely she'll just give up and go park somewhere else.* But the sixth time was the charm.

The woman climbed out and I groaned. It was Emily. She unpacked the baby from the car seat, and looked fearfully up toward my apartment building. She actually spotted me in the window, and I waved, feeling less than enthused.

Why was she here?

I slipped on some sweatpants and a sports jacket and ran down stairs. I'd learned the hard way not to give out the entry code willy-nilly.

She was already standing under the awning when I reached the door. I opened it and stepped back. "Emily! What are you doing here?" More shock than I meant came through my tone. Her baby smiled at me and gurgled, melting my heart.

"I'm sorry. I'm on my way to my mom's. I know, this is terribly intrusive. I just wanted to show you something."

I was about to ask her how she knew where I lived, when I realized that Gainesville, even though it had its busy streets and traffic jams, was still a small town at heart.

"Do you want to come inside? I have to warn you, my place is four floors up."

"Oh, no. I can just show you right here."

She passed over a manila envelope. It was soggy, and she blushed as I took it. "Sorry. It's been outside a few days."

Her baby lunged for it, and I smiled. Carefully, I opened it and peeked inside. At the bottom was a dark piece of paper. I reached in, my nose wrinkling at the feel of the clammy paper, and slid it out.

It appeared to be a magazine article. Gently, I tried to smooth the damp paper.

"I found it by our front porch," she said. "What does it mean?"

The headline was bold. I flinched as I read it. **Why Flintlocks surpassed Firelocks.** The article cut off about two-thirds of the way through. I flipped it over to see if the article continued, but that was an article about a pair of rare pistols. In tiny print along the top right corner, it said, Antique Guns and Ammo.

I swallowed hard. "You found this on your porch?"

"By it," she explained. "Behind the trash can that was up against the railing. I was moving it when I saw it there."

I held the paper with two fingers as though it were a dirty tissue. Honestly, it felt that way to me. Was this proof Terry had known about the musket? Why on earth did she give it to me? "Okay, thank you. I'll figure out what to do with it. Uh, so you're leaving town now?"

She nodded, her curly hair bobbing like it hadn't seen a brush in a few days. "You have my number if you find anything out. You'll call me, right?" She stared earnestly at me.

"Of course I will," I assured her. The baby reached out to me and I gave him my finger to hold. Cute kid.

We said our goodbyes, with me wishing her a safe trip. I

watched her walk away for a moment before I headed back up to my apartment.

After locking the door behind me, I looked at the article again. What in the world was I supposed to do with this? I sighed and laid it flat on the counter to dry, then got ready to head to Cecelia's.

When I arrived, there were only two cars were left in the driveway. I assumed at least two of the guests had already checked out.

The front yard of the Baker Street Bed and Breakfast was starting to resemble how I was feeling inside. Dark, dreary, and wilted. Winter was descending with a vengeance. While we hadn't gotten snow yet, we did have the mucky wet grass, rotting leaves, and overcast sky. I almost couldn't wait for the snow to cover it all up and make everything appear pristine and clean.

A barking dog jolted me out of my reverie.

Peanut.

The puffy Pomeranian came running, but this time she wasn't alone. Oscar was with her, bundled in an old tweed coat and red-and-black checked scarf, carrying the lunch dishes. Peanut, satisfied with her sniffing travels around my feet, ran off to examine a blowing leaf.

"Hi, Oscar. You feeling better?"

He handed me the bowl and plate. "I'm feeling like I have an attic full of squirrels," was his grumpy answer. He stared at his roof with his brow lowered into a deep frown.

"An attic...?" I tried to figure it out. "Do you have a headache?"

"No, I mean my real attic. And they're conspiring to rob me blind in my sleep."

"How do you know?"

"I can hear them. Squeak! Squeak! Squeak! And when I opened my trap door, a couple nuts fell out."

My eyebrows flew up. "How on earth did they get into the attic?"

"Those darn vents right there, I'm thinking." He pointed, his fingers thick and curved with arthritis. He harrumphed. "I figure I'm calling them Dopey, Mopey, and Cotton Tail."

I smiled despite myself. "I'll talk to Frank about it. Do you know him? He's Cecelia's grandson. Maybe he can come help."

"Help? I don't need any help. I'll figure it out. Maybe have a nice squirrel stew tonight."

"Hm, I heard squirrel meat is high in cholesterol," I quoted a line from one of my favorite movies.

He turned to me and stared, unbelievingly. "You think I'm worried about cholesterol?"

"No, I'm just kidding. It's from a—"

"I'm telling you what. You kids with your new-fangled dieting tips. In my day, we ate sticks of butter with every meal. And asked for seconds!"

I didn't know what to say to that. Time to disengage. "Well, I'll let Frank know anyway. He might have a trap, or something else that would work."

His eyebrows rose. "A trap?"

"Then we can move them away from your house."

"Fine. You trap them, you keep them. I never cared for squirrel stew, anyway." His voice faded into a mumble as he started back across his yard. "Bear! Bear!" More grumbling and then, "Peanut! Come!" The little dog looked up from her leaf, tongue lolling out, and raced over. He shuffled back into his house.

I watched him go, and then walked into the B&B. It was peaceful inside, with soft music playing in the background. Thanksgiving was coming soon, a quiet time for the B&B. But then, as Christmas approached, business would start back up again, with people wanting to celebrate someplace else.

"GiGi?" Cecelia called. She must have heard the front door shut.

"Yeah! I'm here!" I walked back to the kitchen, where I found her sitting at the table with a steaming mug. "How are things? Who's left?" I started washing the bowl, knowing I had a long day ahead of me flipping the B&B for the next guests.

"Two of the businessmen checked out. The Laceys and Charles are still here."

I nodded as I helped myself to a cup of coffee.

"How are you doing today? Did you sleep well?" Cecelia asked.

I shrugged as I brought my mug over to the table. Cecelia had out a plate of gingersnaps and was dunking one in her coffee. I helped myself to a cookie and did the same.

"Okay, I guess," I said. "It's sick, but I keep seeing that poor man's eyes and then hearing Terry beg me for help." I sighed and shook my head, remembering. "His wife, Emily, showed up at my place this morning."

"Oh, really? What on earth did she want?"

"She wanted to show me a magazine article. She was on the way to her mother's with the baby."

"A magazine article?"

I shrugged, not wanting to go into it yet.

"Well, at least she's going to her mom's. Good place for her."

"Honestly, I'm relieved. This whole thing surrounding Patrick Armstrong has gotten icky. With lawsuits, extortion..."

"You mean with the gym teacher and the gambling debt?" Cecelia pursed her lips. "Frank mentioned that. It's a shame and distasteful."

"Yes, well, it's also illegal since he stole from the school. So is breaking into someone's house, whether they are alive or not. I'm afraid this murder is going to tear our whole community apart." I sighed.

Cecelia was apparently worried about the same thing, and we sat in silence.

Just then, a familiar face poked his head through the doorway. "Well, I guess I'm taking off!" Charles Vanderstill said, his handsome face breaking into a grin.

"Hey, I'm sorry about how your stay ended. I really

appreciate the info you gave me about the muskets." I said. "It was helpful."

"Oh, no worries. I'd say these things happen. But they really don't."

I nodded in agreement. Not a lot to add to that.

He studied me for a second before digging in his wallet. After a moment, he plucked out a business card. "You have a pen?"

I found one in the junk drawer and passed it over. He scribbled on the back of the card and then handed it over to me. "Here, take this. If you ever have more questions, feel free to call. The number on the front goes straight to the museum, but I put my personal number on the back."

I studied the card, and then flipped it over. "Wow! That's cool that you work there. I bet you get to see a ton of interesting antiques."

"I do, and I love it. I feel like it's my life's duty, above all else, to preserve our history." Charles dipped his head with a cheesy grin.

I nodded, understanding that passion. "I'm sorry we weren't able to make more of your time here."

"Well, it ended up working out. I actually got a call that I'm needed back at the museum, anyway." He offered a hand and I shook it.

"Until next time, then!" He waved and headed out.

"What a nice group of people we had this time," Cecelia said. She dunked another cookie as I again sat across from her. Her phone rang. I listened to her discussing details for Patrick's memorial service being held in two days. I took another sip of my coffee. She thanked the person, and told them that we'd be there, which made me wince. This would be the first one I'd attend since Derek had died. I didn't know what I was going to do.

Unfortunately, the decision was made for me.

CHAPTER 11

*J*ust then, my cell rang too. I answered, fully expecting to hear the same information that Cecelia had just received. "Hello?"

"Is this Georgina Tanner?" The deep voice on the other end caught my attention and I sat up.

"Yes. Who's this?"

"This is Detective Preston from the Gainesville Sheriff's Office. I met you at the crime scene. You're a historian, is that correct?"

"Yes. In some sense of the word." I blushed at my stretch of the truth. Okay, it was a lie. But maybe it would be useful to Terry.

"You mentioned the difference with the muskets. Well, we have another situation involving Patrick Armstrong. I'm wondering if you could meet me at the Armstrong house as a consultant."

"When do you want to meet?" I asked, thinking about the all the beds to be made and laundry done.

"I'm here at the house now, as a matter of fact."

"I see. Now would be good, I guess. I'll be right over."

"That would be much appreciated. Thank you." The call was abruptly disconnected.

Sighing, I rubbed my temples. Cecelia was staring at me with an expectant look on her face.

"Well?" she said, not even giving me a chance. "Who was that?"

"That was the esteemed Detective Preston."

"Esteemed, huh? By who?"

"By himself, apparently. On the day of Armstrong's murder, he kind of downplayed a comment I made about a possible third suspect that could have tampered with the muskets. But now he wants me to come over to the Armstrong house as a consultant."

"Well, maybe he's changed his mind."

I shrugged. "He obviously needs me for some reason. But I can't think of why." I grabbed my jacket. "I'll be back soon. Just leave the bedrooms for me to clean. But, if you want to do the bathrooms...."

She laughed and waved a dishcloth. "Get out of here and leave the toilets to me."

TWENTY MINUTES LATER, I pulled into Patrick's driveway. There was a police car already there, along with another plain-looking blue Toyota. A stocky man in an oversized sweater and baggy blue jeans stood by the front door talking to Detective Preston.

As I walked up, I noticed the broken window had been boarded up.

"Hi there." My words came out in white puffs. I gave an easy grin, zipping up my coat.

"Ms. Georgina Tanner?" Detective Preston asked, his breath similarly steaming.

"Call me Georgie," I amended.

The detective gave a quick nod. He didn't wear anything but his uniform jacket over his shirt. I shivered in my coat, not understanding how he wasn't cold.

Detective Preston continued, "This is Christopher Armstrong, brother to the late Patrick Armstrong." He turned to the stocky man. "And this is the historian I was telling you about, Georgie Tanner. She gave us a heads-up on the weapon used the other day, and is an antique specialist. I thought she could be of some help with the piece you said was missing from your brother's house."

The man's face froze for a moment, as if he were having a slight moment of panic, before he recovered and gave me a tight smile, highlighting his double chin. "Yes, uh, the police called me yesterday after the break in. They wanted me to come down and verify if anything was missing."

He shifted uncomfortably and I noticed his sneakers were nearly worn out. "Honestly, I wouldn't know if most of his stuff were there or not. But I know my brother had an antique, a weapon of some sort. He'd been really excited about it, said it was worth a lot of money. But otherwise, he didn't give me a lot of detail. Just that, 'for my own good,' he was going to be vague. So, when I went through the house to check, I didn't see anything like that. I was hoping, with your expertise, you might come inside and see if there's anything matching that description that I missed."

I nodded. I wasn't so sure I'd be able to find a hidden treasure, but I was up for looking.

"You're the one that caught the person who broke in yesterday?" Christopher asked me.

"Yes, but the man didn't have anything in his hands when I saw him."

"We checked the surrounding area. Doesn't look like the perpetrator hid anything. All he seemed to be concerned with was some documents." Detective Preston chewed the inside of his cheek.

With that, the detective opened the front door. I followed the two men into the house. The interior lighting was dim, with old 70s drapes drawn closed over every window.

The house had a certain odor too. I couldn't quite put my finger on it. Maybe it was a combination of the musty smell of a basement, mixed with cooked ramen noodles.

Detective Preston flipped on the lights. The living room walls were dark with wood paneling. Bookshelves, the type made from particle board, lined one wall. All of the shelves were different degrees of sagging under the weight of books that were stacked both vertically and horizontally to fill every last square inch of space. On the floor was an overflow of two more piles of books.

I read some of the titles. Most of the books were nonfiction. Patrick definitely had a love for history. But nothing there stood out to me as being an antique.

I wandered the room some more. A large oak desk squatted against another wall. I walked to desk, my gaze bouncing over the scattered papers, pen jar, check register, and more books that covered the top. Hanging on the wall above the desk was a wood-framed photograph.

I leaned forward to study the picture. It was a newspaper article, dated six years prior. The image in the article was of two flintlock pistols sitting in a wooden case. The article described the pair as George Washington's saddle pistols, worth nearly two million dollars. The article stated that someone had actually picked them up during an estate sale, and now no one knew where the pistols were.

Hmmm. I stepped back and studied the desk. There were six large drawers, three on each side. One of them was slightly ajar. I grabbed a pen from the jar and used it to open the drawer more.

Inside was a piece of fabric that had been scrunched as if to cushion something. In the center was a clear rectangle imprint of an object that had been stored there for years.

Suddenly, I had a bad feeling.

"Right here," I pointed. Detective Preston glanced inside. "Something was taken from this drawer."

"And you think it was valuable?" he asked. He bounced on his toes as his eyes lit up.

"I think it was that." I tapped the picture with my pen. "The case looks to be the same shape as that indent."

He glanced between the picture and the fabric imprint. "Or it was a lock box, a cigar box, or even a really nifty pencil box. I'll make note of it, but let's keep looking in case something else stands out to you."

Christopher leaned in to examine the drawer himself. "You think that's where he kept the guns? He'd had to have had insurance on them, right? Should I make a claim?" His voice rose with eagerness.

I stared at him, and his definitive use of guns. He caught my gaze and blanched. His forehead looked sweaty. "I mean, uh, if that's what was in there."

He was lying to me. I knew it. But why lie about knowing what the valuable thing was that Patrick had?

"There's another consideration," I said. "Maybe he felt threatened and moved the item for some reason."

"So, you're saying they're somewhere else?" Christopher's

gaze jumped about the room. "Because he thought someone was going to take them?"

"Or maybe he wasn't supposed to have them." I muttered to myself, but the brother's face jerked toward me, his eyes wide.

"Why would you say that?" he asked.

Realizing there was something else going on, and not wanting to tip off the brother, I shook my head. "Like Detective Armstrong said, it could have just been a pencil box."

As I said it, I had to try hard not to allow my eyes to move up to the photograph framed on the wall.

Christopher shifted, uneasy. He cracked his knuckles and licked his bottom lip, fat and blubbery. Something about him set my teeth on edge. He did say that he didn't get along with his brother.

If Patrick truly had those pistols, and Christopher knew they were here, that was a serious motive.

A brother murdering a brother. It had been known to happen before.

"How long have you been in town?" I asked. "Were you at the reenactment?" I tried to infuse as much pity and worry into my voice as possible, to seem compassionate as I fished for information.

Detective Preston watched us. He may have caught on to what I was trying to do.

"I flew in last night. No, I wasn't there, thankfully. I know I said we weren't close, but that would have been devastating for me."

"It would have been horrible. I am very sorry for your loss."

He nodded, his lips pressed together grimly. We stood quietly for a moment. I hoped the empty space would encourage Christopher to say something more, but it dragged on and on. Finally, I was at the edge of breaking the silence myself, when Detective Preston cleared his throat. "Shall we continue?"

The detective led the way through the kitchen and then the two bedrooms. My skin crawled while standing in Patrick's bedroom. His blankets were still flung back from when he'd gotten up yesterday morning, with various pieces of clothing strewn about. Detective Preston swept a flashlight beam through the closet and under the bed. He pulled out the dresser drawers. My stomach rolled with nausea.

But other than historical pieces of art on the walls, I didn't see anything else that caught my interest or seemed so obviously displaced as that empty spot in the desk drawer.

When he'd finished his search, Detective Preston looked at me expectantly.

I shrugged. "Well, you know my thoughts. I think he had those pistols. They fit with the hush-hush conversation that Christopher described earlier. And if there was a chance he wasn't suppose to have them, then he'd probably not want to give any more information than 'I have something valuable.'"

"And you have no idea where they could be?" the detective asked.

"There's still one place left we can look," I said with a confident nod.

CHAPTER 12

*B*oth men watched me with interest. I bit my lip, not liking the spotlight.

"Well, has anyone searched his classroom?" I asked.

Detective Preston's eyebrows flickered. "That's next on my list. You must be a mind reader. You want to tag along?"

I nodded. Why not? I might as well see this through.

"What about me?" Christopher asked, his voice whining. His head swiveled between the two of us.

My nails bit into my palms as I clenched my hands. *Please tell him no.* I didn't think I could hang around him another minute. Something about him made my skin crawl.

Luckily, the detective didn't let me down. "This is official police business. We'll keep in touch and let you know of anything we find," he said, with a no-nonsense dip of his head.

Christopher seemed to wilt before us, but he didn't try to argue. We left him staring at the desk, with the detective giving a stern command that if Christoper should find anything, he needed to alert the police department at once, as it could be evidence for the murder investigation.

As I walked out to my van, I couldn't help but glance over at Terry Brooks' place. The driveway was empty and the windows dark with Emily gone. I checked out the tree. Detective Preston joined me.

"Hard to believe this would be at the center of all that," he said. "Shame how depraved people can be."

I nodded, stuffing my hands into my jacket's pockets. It was cold, with that icy touch to the breeze that threatened a snowfall.

Detective Preston must have felt it too. He rubbed his hands together. "All right, quit dawdling. Let's get going."

Dawdling, huh? I bit back my retort and got into the van.

The trip to the school was uneventful to the outside eye, but my stomach clenched. I wasn't sure if I was about to be a part of solving one of the greatest historical mysteries of the

American Revolution: finding George Washington's saddle pistols.

Would this be enough to prove there could have been other suspects besides Terry? Could Terry walk free even though he was the one who pulled the musket trigger? Or was my entire idea about to go down the drain?

The school's parking lot was overflowing from all of the students' cars. I drove around back to where I remembered the teachers had their own spots.

Detective Preston didn't follow me, choosing instead to park in front of the entrance. By the time I had my van parked, and was hurrying up the sidewalk to meet him, he already had a crowd of kids gathered around his vehicle, interested to see why he was here.

As I approached, I heard him saying, "Why aren't you guys in class? No, there's nothing happening here that concerns any of you. Hey! You! Don't be touching my car, or you better believe it will concern you."

Mrs. Matthews, the principal, walked out. "All right, everyone. Excitement's over. Get back to class." She waited with her arms crossed until the last of the stragglers was through the door, then she stepped closer to the detective. "What's going on?"

"I'm Detective Preston, investigating Patrick Armstrong's

murder. I'd like to take a look at his classroom, or any other place he may have kept his personal items. This right here is Georgie Tanner, my consultant."

Mrs. Matthews smiled at me. "I know who she is."

I blanched under her smile. It had been nearly fourteen years since I'd graduated from here and I dreaded to think of what she remembered of me. There was that one time when I worked with my marketing class to move all of the classroom's furniture up to the roof in the middle of the night, ending with a trip to the police station for me.

"Hello." I smiled and tried not to bite my lip.

"Move any furniture recently?" she asked, a dimple dipping in slightly.

I chuckled. "Not too much lately."

She nodded briskly, fun time over. "Class is in session, so I'd appreciate it if you both would be as inconspicuous as possible."

I nodded, while Detective Preston answered, "Of course."

We followed her into the high school. Memories hit like a tidal wave. Standing in the foyer was surreal. Had thirteen years really passed since I'd last been here? The same scents filled the air; greasy cafeteria pizza, tater-tots, teenage sweat and the subsequent clouded-mixture of body spray. The lockers were in the same state of disrepair with their peeling paint and dented doors.

We passed the glass case that gleamed with trophies that I remembered. New linoleum had been installed since I'd attended, but even that didn't look new, with a worn trail down the center where everyone walked. The sight of the walls around the classroom doors brought nostalgia, covered as they were with posters about upcoming plays, student government issues, and dances.

Mrs. Matthews led us down the left wing, her sensible brown square heels clapping on the floor. It was clear which door belonged to Mr. Armstrong's classroom. It was covered with sympathy cards and homemade posters. I was a bit surprised, remembering how he was unliked.

But death and grief can bring back only the best memories about a person.

Mrs. Matthews tapped on the door. A minute later, it opened and a harried-looking older woman came out. Her eyes widened when she saw Detective Preston, quickly glancing between him and the principal

"Yes?" she said, nervously plucking at the edge of her sweater.

"How are you doing?" Mrs. Matthews asked. "I know we threw you like a steak to the lions, having to sub for Mr. Armstrong in this difficult situation."

"It's bearable." The substitute gave what I'd call a brave smile. "They're obviously having a hard time."

Mrs. Matthews nodded sympathetically. "Ms. Cooper, this is Detective Preston. He needs a few minutes in your classroom. What are the students doing right now?"

I heard shouts from inside and had a feeling the teens were doing anything but what they were supposed to be doing.

Apparently Mrs. Matthews felt the same way. Her eyebrows furrowed at a particularly piercing scream, and she opened the door.

"Ladies and gentlemen," she said as she walked in, her steps firm. The effect in the classroom was immediate. I peeked in behind her to see expressions of shock on the students' faces at the appearance of the principal. Several quietly returned to their seats. Most seemed to have developed an intense interest in the books before them.

You could hear a pin drop.

"Glad to see everyone is working. Please don't let us disturb your studies," Mrs. Matthews said in a stern tone. She stepped to the side to allow Detective Preston and me into the room.

Every windowsill and available flat surface was covered with cards and stuffed animals. Condolences were written on the chalkboard. It made me question if there was more to him, despite the rumors.

The rest of the classroom had been decorated by Patrick with posters depicting different historical scenes and quotes. I glanced over them, searching for any clues. Detective Preston walked to Armstrong's desk and began to search.

Behind the desk, to the left of the chalkboard, stood a filing cabinet. I pulled open a drawer and started digging. It mostly had worksheets, lesson plans, maps, not of interest. I would find the same thing in the rest of them.

In the meantime, Detective Preston was making quick work through the desk drawers. The bottom right one was locked. That grabbed both our attention. I left the filling cabinet and walked over.

"You have a key for this?" he asked the principal. She shook her head. I bent over to try it. No luck. Something made me check the top drawer. There was a box of staples, and I looked inside. Opening it revealed a small metal key.

Detective Preston smiled, seeing it in my hand.

"Cecelia uses the same trick," I explained. I glanced up and saw a few students watching us. I continued quieter, "Only not a staple box. She hides the spare key in a box of matches."

I slid the key into the lock and turned it gently. It made a clicking sound, jolting me with excitement, and the drawer was unlocked. Slowly, I opened it, my heart thumping in my chest. This was it! I could feel it!

I about fell over in a dead faint when the nose of a pistol came into view.

CHAPTER 13

"*W*hat the...." Detective Preston whistled.

Adrenaline pumped through me. I could feel my pulse as I opened the door completely.

But, it was a few seconds later when I realized it was a replica. Carefully, I pointed to the grip.

"This is plastic. It's fake, a prop," I murmured to the detective.

"It may be fake, but I'm furious that he would have kept such a thing in his classroom," Mrs. Mathews fumed.

What lay underneath the gun was just a bunch more papers and some tests that Patrick apparently hadn't graded yet.

With a sigh, I shut the drawer, and it locked again with a

click. Disappointment took me down the rollercoaster just as fast as excitement had taken me up.

I started to close the top center drawer, too. But as it was closing, a noise made me pause. Call it a hunch, but I reopened the door and searched for the source. There was a folded piece of paper standing on end and dragging against the drawer guide.

I plucked it out. Impatiently, I unfolded it and a business card fell out. Preston picked up the card and handed it over. As I read it, I recognized it right away. I had one in my own wallet. What in the world?

I reached into my purse and pulled out an identical business card. Charles had given it to me just before he'd checked out of the bed and breakfast.

What did this mean? Okay, take a second. Think. "Charles was a guest at the bed and breakfast," I said.

The detective took both of the business cards to compare. I closed my eyes and squeezed my temples with my fingers.

"Museum of American History," Detective Preston read. "Doesn't seem that unusual that a curator would connect with the history teacher, now does it?"

Actually, he was right. Relief flooded through me. For a

second there, I'd been panicked, thinking I'd brought the killer to the reenactment to watch his victim die.

The detective turned the card over. "Look at this." He shoved it my way. On the back, scribbled in pen, was a note: *Don't trust Draken. Call Charles.* And then a phone number.

Who was the message for? Patrick? It was in his drawer. And who was Mr. Draken?

I shook my head. "That's Charles' number. I have no idea who Mr. Draken is," I confessed. The phone number matched the number Charles had written on the back of my card.

"I guess I'll be giving Charles a call then," Detective Preston said, frowning. He glanced at Mrs. Matthews. "Thank you for your time. I think we've got everything we need here."

"I'll walk you out," she said.

We passed the substitute teacher, who did not look at all confident at being left alone once again with the students.

Mrs. Matthews paused at the doorway. "Oh, and Ms. Cooper. I'll be patrolling the halls for the next hour, should you need me."

Ms. Cooper flushed with gratitude. "I'm sure we'll be fine."

The principal gave her a nod and we left the room.

Ten minutes later, as I sat in the van's driver's seat, my thoughts began to churn again. As far as I knew, my customer hadn't met the teacher. He didn't seem to recognize him at the field. So how had the teacher gotten his card? And what were they meeting about?

I pulled out my smartphone and typed in the web address for the New York City museum. I needed to learn more about it, since this was the second time I'd run across its name. They had wings dedicated to different time periods of the United States history. What interested me the most was the wing that advertised that they specialized in Revolutionary weaponry and war memorabilia.

A flashing red banner on the home page informed visitors of a new and surprising exhibit opening up in the next few days.

A rare antique from our first president. Sign up now to be the first to hear of it!

My heart sank. That must have meant the George Washington's saddle pistols had been found. But how? And at what cost? Were they sold by Patrick Armstrong to the museum, donated by him, or did he ever have them to begin with?

I stuck the keys into the ignition and started the van. A snowflake landed on the windshield and then another. I looked out my side window to the sky. The clouds were dark, roiling along the horizon. It was going to get ugly out soon. Old Bella didn't do so well in the slick and the ice. I needed to get back to Cecelia's and finish cleaning, and then get my butt home.

By the time I got to the Baker Street Bed and Breakfast, the snow was sticking. I groaned as I got out of the van, bummed to see my wet footprints in the thin layer of the snow. I hurried up to the porch, noticing Frank's police car was already parked along the side.

"Honey! I'm home!" I joked as I stamped my feet on the welcome mat.

"Hi, GiGi," Cecelia called from the living room. I peeked in there to see her in her favorite armchair, feet propped up. There was a fire going in the fireplace, with a big stack of firewood. I guessed Frank had probably chopped it and brought it in.

Speaking of Frank, there he was glowering at me over the top of a brandy glass.

"What's with you?" I asked, flopping down in a chair across from Cecelia.

"What's with me is that I got roped into changing all the beds in this place, while you ran off doing detective stuff. I'd like to know how that happened." He scowled.

"It's already done?" I looked at Cecelia.

She smiled, her cheeks pink from the roaring fire, and nodded in confirmation. "All done, dusted, and ready!"

Wow, this day just got immensely better. I smiled at Frank.

"You look like the Cheshire cat, smiling like that," he said. "Now, are you going to explain to me what happened?"

"Sure," I examined my fingernails nonchalantly. "I was called because the detective wanted an *expert* opinion. Of course, he thought of me."

Frank snorted and tossed back the rest of his drink. It made him cough and I watched him with concern. A fragment of shrapnel lay in his chest from an IED bomb that ended his tour in Afghanistan. Winters were hard on him. He took a few deep breaths, his face red. It made me sad, both of us in our early thirties, to see him struggle like that.

"You okay?" I asked.

He waved me off. "Grandma, I'm going to make a sandwich and then head home." He got up and walked into the kitchen.

Him mentioning food made me kind of hungry too. I realized I hadn't eaten all day. "I guess, I'll make myself one too," I told Cecelia.

"You go help yourself. I'm too plumb worn out to make

dinner tonight."

"Want me to make you one?" I asked.

"No. I had a bowl of soup earlier. I'm feeling pretty good, but thank you." She closed her eyes and smiled. The fire crackled, joining the soft music she always kept playing in the background. I could see she was feeling pretty content. Did my heart good to see her smile like that.

When I walked into the kitchen, Frank already had out the bread and lunch meat. He was still rummaging in the fridge.

"What are you looking for?" I asked.

"Huh?" His head poked out, mayonnaise in hand. "We have any pickles?"

"There's a new jar in the pantry. Here, let me get them."

I opened the pantry door to search for the pickles. Darn it all, they were on the top shelf. I stared at them for a second, not even trying to reach for them. With a sigh, I started for the kitchen chair to carry it over and climb up.

"Need help, shorty?"

I mockingly glared at him before giving him a smile. By the time I reached the chair, he already had the pickles down. "Here you go, munchkin."

"Oh, you're a funny one, today," I said.

He grabbed a knife from the drawer while I snagged some mustard and shut the fridge.

At the table, he made room for me. "Mustard, yuck."

"Yeah, well that's how I feel about that mayonnaise." I sliced a few pickles and offered them to him. He pushed the lunch meat package towards me. As we worked, I filled him in about the two business cards.

"Preston going to call them tomorrow?" he asked, shoving an extra piece of ham in his mouth.

"I assume so. Too bad the museum is closed tonight, already. Do you like Preston?"

Frank nodded. "He's descent. But I'm better." His lips lifted at the corner.

"Always so humble," I said with a chuckle.

"Can't be humble about the truth." He picked up his sandwich and took a big bite. I noticed his hand went to rub the scar on his chest.

"How are you feeling?"

He shrugged. "Not my favorite time of year." With that, he pointed toward the window with his sandwich, where I saw the snow falling harder than ever.

I took a bite and chewed quickly. I needed to get home.

CHAPTER 14

The next morning, I woke up with the excited shivers, like it was the start of summer vacation, just waiting to hear back from Detective Parker about his phone call with the museum. Those missing muskets had given me another hard night's sleep, thinking about them.

And the more I thought, the more I hoped the muskets hadn't actually been found. My only goal was to get Terry out of jail. I needed to prove to Detective Parker that the motive behind Armstrong's death was not revenge, but greed for a historical treasure.

I got up and stumbled into the kitchen to make some coffee. I laughed when I caught sight of my face reflecting in the microwave door. My hair was sticking up on one side, like I'd gone to bed in a cyclone.

While waiting for the coffee to perk, my gaze landed on the magazine page that Emily had brought over the day before. It was dry now. I picked it up and reread it, oddly irritated at how the article cut off. I flipped it over even though I knew the article didn't continue on the other side. I did it for the same reason I checked the fridge for the third time in a night, as if something good to eat might magically appear.

Well, my wishful thinking paid off for the first time ever. Staring at me in bold print was the exact thing I'd wished to see.

President's Missing Pistols a National Treasure.

I'd been so blinded by the flintlock article, terrified that it might somehow tie Terry to the murder, that I hadn't paid attention to the other side. I realized that this was the article that was supposed to be shared, not the other one. Quickly, I read it. I finished just as my coffee pot burped its last drops. Thoughtfully, I poured myself a mug. The article hadn't shared anything new, just that the George Washington saddle pistols were thought to be in a collector's home.

I carried my mug and phone to the couch and sat down. After checking my phone for a message from Detective Parker, I finally gave in to my curiosity. Call me snoopy, I didn't care. I couldn't wait any longer.

I rang up the Museum of United States History.

A chipper man answered on the third ring. "Museum of United States History, how can I help you?"

"Hi there. Is there any way to reach Charles Vanderstill? He's a curator there."

"Our curator's numbers are private. They only give them out to who they wish. I'm sorry, we don't have extensions. But maybe I can help you."

I'd just have to used the number he'd written down then. "I noticed the banner on your main page advertising a coming exhibit. Is there more information on what it will be and when the exhibit will be occurring?"

The peppy tone continued, "Absolutely. The antique comes from the Colonial Era. We've been tracking it down for quite some time, and are quite honored to finally be in the process of acquiring the item."

"How did you guys find it? Can you give me a hint at what it is?"

"The museum is under a confidentiality agreement, and as such, the donor's name is anonymous. We'd like to keep everything as a surprise to reveal on the big day."

"Are we talking about the George Washington saddle pistols?"

His voice lost some of its joviality. "I'm not at liberty to discuss any additional details. As you can imagine, many people are seeking them. We can't reveal too much more until the pieces make it in, making sure that full security protocols are in place to protect them. Once we have the pieces at our facility and secured, we will be releasing more information about the exhibit."

"So they aren't even at the museum yet?"

"Ma'am, exactly why are you asking this?" The receptionist sounded wary. I realized I probably came across as the very type of person that would be looking to intercept the artifacts.

"Actually, I was wondering who the benefactor was. I got a card for the museum from Mr. Vanderstill, who I met earlier, and I wondered if he was working with the donor."

"I'm sorry, but I would suggest you call curator directly."

"Okay, I understand. Thank you anyway."

"Take care and come visit us anytime."

I hung up the phone and snagged the business card from my purse. Patrick Armstrong had the same one, with a second name on the back. After hesitating for a second, I called Frank.

"What do you want?" Cheery as always.

"Frank, don't you ever answer the phone with a hello? And why sound so suspicious? I could be calling to let you know that I'm coming over with a dozen homemade cookies."

"Hello. And I know you. You don't bake. Now what do you want?"

I kind of bristled at his comment that I didn't bake. Made me want to whip out my recipe book right now.

Except I didn't own a recipe book. But I was going to change that.

I cleared my throat. "I want to know if you can do some recognizance."

"Weird request. Considering that's what I get paid for," he deadpanned.

"Would you find something out for me? Please."

"What is it?"

"I don't know if Detective Parker's already looking, but I was wondering about the name written on the back of the business card we found yesterday. Is there any way to discover if that name is in Patrick's phone, listed as a contact? The name is Draken. Patrick wrote the note on the back as if he knew him."

"Yeah, I can do that."

"Also, do you know if they're still looking into the quarterback's family? The dad did threaten Patrick that morning. And there's that letter I found."

"Interesting you should bring that up. We confronted Dane, and he denied leaving the note. That's a dead end for now, but we did dig up a little something-something on him. Dane is a musket enthusiast himself. He owns a rifle shop and has his federal firearms license. If there was anyone who could get ahold of a rare musket or replica, it'd be him."

"Really?" My excitement made me jump out of the chair. "You need to see if those high school students can identify him."

"Which ones?"

"The two boys manning the armory table. They mentioned they saw Dane looking at the muskets. But no one has taking me seriously. Maybe he even had an accomplice drop off the musket first, and then he came over to see for himself that it was available on the armory table. Or maybe he did it, himself. The boys said the guy was wearing a hoody. And, that note did basically threaten Patrick's life."

He made a noise that almost sounded like a chuckle and my mouth dropped. Had I finally made him laugh?

"What? What did I say?"

"You caught me off guard, is all. That's pretty smart."

I raised my eyebrows. "You shouldn't be so surprised. I am smart."

"I know you are. It's just been a while, you know." He cleared his throat. "I mean since we talked. I mean, as adults. I still remember you being the bratty kid trying to copy my math homework."

It was my turn to laugh then. "That's true, but your memory's twisted. It was you copying from my homework."

"Yeah. Maybe. Anyway, I'll ask around and let you know what I find."

"Thank you."

"Stay out of trouble." He hung up.

I couldn't help the grin as I set the phone down. He'd thought I was the brat? He was the one who always got me in trouble, acting like the sheriff even back then. Every summer, we'd hung out with a few other neighborhood kids. Really, we just ran wild. Gone after breakfast down to the lake or exploring the woods. Didn't come back until supper time.

He'd always been the serious one in our group. And I'd always liked to tease him.

I chuckled. Maybe I was the brat.

Stretching a bit, I walked over to get some more coffee. After a moment, I decided on a bowl of cereal. I took my haul back to the table, where the painting supplies stared at me. With a groan, I returned to the living room.

Sitting on the coffee table was my purse. After a second, I rifled through and pulled out the business card.

I read the name printed across the front. Charles Vanderstill. Curator. The museum number was printed underneath. I turned it over and looked at his handwritten number on the back. I took a bite and crunched, my thoughts spinning. Should I? He did say to call if I ever had any questions. What could be a bigger question than asking if his museum was acquiring the lost George Washington saddle pistols? Maybe I could figure out how he knew Patrick Armstrong.

After talking myself into it, I dialed the number.

"Hello?" Charles answered on the third ring.

"Hi, Mr. Vanderstill. This is Georgie Tanner from the Baker Street Bed and Breakfast."

There was a pause as he took a second to register my name. And then, "Oh, yes! How are you? Did I leave something behind?"

"No, no. Nothing like that. I just have a quick question. Do you have a moment?"

"For a quick question, sure. Anything longer than that, then I'll have to call you back. I'm on my way to teach a seminar right now."

"Oh, that's great. I, uh, I was requested to help go through Mr. Armstrong's belongings. Do you remember him?"

"Of course. The poor man that was shot. I remember the musket wasn't authentic. Go on."

"Well, I found your business card among his things. I was wondering if he'd been in contact with you."

"Actually, his brother contacted me a few days prior. Christopher is his name, I believe. He asked when we could have a meeting. That he had something beyond my wildest dreams to show me. Well, I've heard that before, but I knew I'd be in the area, so I agreed to meet with him."

"And did you have that meeting?" I asked.

"No. He called that evening and said that, with his brother's death, he needed to reevaluate. Of course, I understood. Terribly tragic. A horrible affair."

"And no word from him on rescheduling the meeting?"

"No. None yet." His words sounded breathless, as though he

were running. "I'm very sorry, Ms. Tanner, but as it happens, I'm late."

"One last thing before you go. Do you know a Mr. Draken?"

"No, sorry. I do not."

"Okay, I'm sorry to have kept you. If you hear from Christopher again, would you let me know? And have a good lecture!"

"Thank you! I will!" With that, he hung up.

I sat back, feeling frustrated. Christopher had called him? But why? Where had he picked up the business card? If he killed his brother for the pistols, wouldn't he be trying to get rid of them now? Instead, he canceled the meeting. What was he waiting for?

Or was it possible that Christopher had found something completely separate from Patrick that he wanted to share?

I groaned as I stared into my coffee. As interesting as all of this was, it was basically a pile of gossip and non-facts. Nothing that would set Terry free.

I stood to rinse my cup. Like a flash, a memory hit me of that day when I'd jumped into the fight to help Terry. I remembered now, as we'd walked to the library, he'd hissed at me. "I'll never let this happen again. They better watch out. If someone tries to bully me again, I'll kill them." The lenses of his glasses had gleamed in the fluorescent light, hiding his eyes.

I shivered. As quickly as I could, I pushed that thought from my mind, wishing I could erase it just as effectively as rinsing my cup.

CHAPTER 15

The name Draken rumbled in my head. Don't trust Draken, the card had said. Why was it in Armstrong's desk at the school? Who else had gone rummaging through that desk?

I pulled up my web browser and did a quick search for the name. The instant I did it, I felt foolish. The search brought up pages and pages of "Drakens." I had no idea how I was going to narrow that down.

I sighed, running my fingers through my hair. I pulled it back into a ponytail, noting that it was probably time for another haircut, since most of my hair fit into it now. I'd once had long hair, down past the half-way point of my back. But I'd cut it when I moved here. I loved my new haircut so much, I'd probably never grow it out again.

So, back to the problem at hand. What was I going to do? I had a few clues, but so far, they'd been useless to me. I was no closer to figuring out if my hunches were right. I didn't even have proof the item missing from Armstrong's drawer was actually the missing Washington pistols, despite what my gut said.

Maybe I just needed to have a talk with Patrick's brother. Bring him some cookies, and see where his head was at. Yeah, he'd creeped me out when I first met him, but it was possible that's just how he dealt with grief.

And me, of all people, should understood grief. Despite my counseling appointments, I still struggled with accepting Derek's death. I think the hardest part for me was that I didn't understand why it had happened. Derek didn't even brake, just swerved off the road and crashed down the cliff.

My eyes fluttered closed. I'd never accept the detectives explanation of what had happened. He'd loved life. He would have never tried to hurt himself. If I could just make sense of why he hadn't tried to stop, maybe I would be able to let go.

Maybe that's what was bothering me so much right now with Patrick's murder. I didn't understand why it'd happened.

With that thought, I grabbed my purse and keys. I knew I was pushing the boundaries to go visit Christopher. But my friend was still in jail, and the police didn't seem to be moving very fast.

Besides, what could it hurt? The man was grieving. A friendly face and a plate of cookies might be helpful.

I started my van, feeling a bit out of breath, having run down all four flights of stairs. Now that I put my mind to it, I wanted to get to the Armstrong house as soon as possible. But my first stop was at the B&B. I was hoping Cecelia would still have some cookies I could snag.

"Soon as possible" quickly defined itself to be twenty miles an hour. The snow had piled up through the night. The snow plows had been out, and the road was salted, but it was still slick enough that I passed more than a few cars that had slid off the road.

I really did not want to get Old Bella stuck. As big as she was, she didn't do the greatest in these driving conditions. I drove carefully in the tracks before me, and tried to stay off both the gas and the brake.

Baker Street was in even worse condition than the main road because the plow didn't come down here. I crept along in the wet tire tracks, thankful I wasn't the first person to drive down it.

I pulled into the driveway and jumped out. The snow crunched under my boots. My breath clouded before me as I gazed into her spacious yard. As I watched, snow slid from a branch on one of the trees and fell with a soft "whump" on the white ground. Tucking my hands into my pockets, I hurried to the front door, where I stomped my feet hard on the mat.

Opening the door immediately immersed me into the sweet scent of vanilla and chocolate. Cecelia definitely had cookies. And they were fresh baked.

"Hey, Auntie," I sang, as I ran in to the kitchen.

"Hi, my lovely. What are you doing on your day off?"

"Actually..." I reached out for a cookie. Perfect chocolate chip, so warm I had to blow on my fingers. "I was hoping you had some cookies available. I was wondering if you'd be okay with me taking some over to Christopher Armstrong. That's Patrick's brother."

"Oh, my goodness! Is he still in town? Of course he is." She answered her own question with a nod. "With the memorial tomorrow. Let me see what I can do."

She bustled about in the fridge, and soon filled a small casserole dish with leftovers. I watched two pork chops, a scoop of potatoes with a spoonful of gravy, and broccoli go in the dish. She wrapped it in foil, and then crammed a plate full with cookies. With efficiency born from years of experience, she packed all of this into a basket and handed it over. "You take this to that poor man. Tell him on behalf of the Baker Street Bed and Breakfast, we are so sorry for his loss."

"Aw." I gave her a big hug. I could well understand why my grandma had been her best friend. She was such a kind woman. "Thank you. I'll let him know."

Carrying the basket with me, I headed back out into the slush and snow. Old Bella started up with the usual plume of exhaust, and we were off for the Armstrong place.

I thought about calling to let him know I was on my way, when I realized I didn't have his phone number. Honestly, Cecelia's open heart and generosity made me feel kind of guilty for having any suspicious thoughts toward Patrick's brother. The poor guy had to come in from out of town to deal with his brother's affects. He probably didn't know a soul here. I didn't even know if he'd have someone to sit with tomorrow during the memorial.

Well, if I saw him alone, I'd sit with him, if he wanted.

I pulled into the Armstrong driveway. There were no other cars around and the house windows were dark. Knocking on the door confirmed what I'd feared, there was no one home. I had to admit, I was pretty disappointed.

I thought for a second about leaving the food on the porch,

but I could only imagine the size of the squirrel attack there would be on the food.

Which reminded me, I needed to talk to Frank about setting up some squirrel traps for Oscar.

I carried the basket to the van and set it in the passenger seat, and then pulled out my cell phone.

—Hey Frank, I have a big favor to ask.

I dropped the phone into the cup holder, not able to help my smile at picturing the look on his face when he heard he was needed as the great squirrel re-locater.

A popping sound made me look up. What was that? No. Not popping... crackling. I sat straighter in the driver's seat, trying to see.

Smoke. Just the tiniest curl, but it was definitely leaking out of the house window before me.

CHAPTER 16

The hair on the back of my neck rose. Quickly, I scrambled for my phone and called 911.

"911. What's your emergency?" a cool, calm voice answered, sounding exactly the opposite of what I felt.

"There's a house fire! I'm parked right in front!"

"What's the residence address?"

I had no idea. I glanced around but none of the houses were marked. Quickly, I scrambled out of the van and ran to the corner to find the street sign. I gave the street address, and then for good measure, I threw in, "It's Patrick Armstrong's place!" I had no idea if the operator would know who Patrick was or not. It's amazing how panic can addle one's thinking. I ran back to the van.

"Is there anyone inside the residence?"

I strained to see through the windows. Now I could actually see flames licking the inside of the glass. "No cars in the driveway. I don't think there's anyone inside, but I don't know for sure."

"Please move your vehicle to a safe place and remain inside. Help is on the way."

I hung up, my hands trembling. I couldn't believe it. Smoke now billowed from the back of the house. The sight spurred me into movement and I jumped into the van. I started it and pulled forward.

It took me a second before I realized the van drove funny. Wobbly. I thought panic was making me feel things that weren't there, but by the time I'd driven halfway down the street, I realized something was very wrong.

After I was sure I was a safe distance away and wouldn't be in the path of the fire trucks, I pulled the van over. I climbed out, staring at the house. Smoke swelled over the roof the Armstrong place. "Come on. Come on." I could hardly stand it, just waiting there, helpless, for the firefighters to come.

I glanced down at my tire, remembering the weird driving. My mouth dropped open.

The tire was slashed. Not a little nail hole, but an actual gash that left the van resting on the metal rim.

How on earth could this have happened? Did I drive over some glass?

I ran my fingers through my hair. Okay, I need to call road assistance. There was no way I could drive on it any further.

An explosion of glass made me jump. The front windows had blown out of Patrick's house. The flames were eating through the roof and the overhanging branches of the black walnut tree had started to smoke.

I turned toward Terry's house, feeling helpless. His snow-covered roof was dripping on the side nearest to the Armstrongs'. *Please, oh please. Let help get here in time. Don't let Terry lose his house too, not after everything else.*

The black walnut tree seemed to shimmer from the fire's heat. The tiny branches closest to the roof started to shrivel up, like fingers pulling away from a wet hairball.

Sirens came up the road. Relief filled me, an odd feeling since the sound of ambulance sirens nearly always brought a flashback to that horrible night when Derek died. Maybe because every part of me was on sensory overload, all I felt was the sense of rescue.

Two fire trucks turned down the street, followed by an

ambulance. Then one...no, two police cars came behind, the second police car screeching around the corner.

I watched them park and started walking toward them. The second police car drove past the house and parked right in the middle of the street. The door flew open and Frank jumped out.

His face was white and his eyes huge as he stared toward the house. By now, the roar of the fire was amping up, sounding like an approaching train. Firefighters began unwinding the truck's hoses.

"Frank!" I yelled. "Frank! Over here."

He turned, wild eyed, and saw me. I swear, his face crumpled. He pressed his lips together hard as he walked toward me.

"Hey," I said. "You okay?"

He grabbed me and hugged me. Hugged me tighter than I'd been hugged in years. I could hear his deep exhales.

"Hey, what's going on?" I rubbed his back in small circles, feeling his shuddering breaths against me. "You're okay."

"I'm okay." His voice was ironic and warm against my neck. "Georgie, when I got the call and heard the code... I knew the address. They said there was a woman involved. I called my grandma and she said you were here...."

Oh, my gosh. He'd thought I was in the fire, hurt somehow. Maybe worse. I can only imagine what emotion this triggered in him, after all he'd gone through on his tour of duty. This time, I held him, tighter than I'd held anyone in years.

"I'm okay, I'm okay," I whispered, trying to be the strength for his weakness.

I could feel his breathing slow. Finally, he let me go. He draped his arm around me and we turned to look at the house.

The firefighters blasted water at the base of the fire. It was a battle. Eventually, they turned their focus to making sure the fire wouldn't jump to the Brooks' house.

I stood there and watched the tree blaze. The tree that had caused all of this. And I watched the Armstrong house, together with any clues, treasures, or evidence about the George Washington pistols, collapse to the ground.

CHAPTER 17

I can't say I got as warm of a greeting from the other officer. This was Officer Burton, and I met him when I originally met Detective Parker. Apparently, he felt my presence at the house was suspicious, despite the food basket in the back seat of my van.

Lucky for me that Frank was there to vouch for my character. There was a hot minute there where I thought they were about to bring me down. Apparently, seeing my presence at two crime scenes was putting me at the top of the list of suspects.

After taking my statement, the police officer left. The firemen were still at work to make sure there weren't any hot spots left.

Frank walked me back to my van. I shivered. My jacket was zipped as high as it could go, and I buried my nose into it.

Frank clapped my shoulder. "You cold?"

"Freezing." Our feet crunched on the compacted snow on the road. About halfway to my van, Frank stopped. He leaned down and picked something out of the snow. His brow wrinkled as he inspected it.

It was a knife. Specifically, a butcher's knife, like the type one kept in the kitchen.

"What the heck is this doing out here?" he asked.

I blamed the cold for how slow my brain was clicking over. But it dawned on me what the knife had been used for. With a groan, I yanked my phone out of my pocket. I dialed roadside assistance, blowing on my fingers as I waited for someone to answer.

Frank looked at me with one eyebrow up. "What's up, kid?"

"My tire got slashed." I pointed to the knife. "I have a good feeling that's what did it."

Frank cursed and trudged back to his car, returning moments later with an evidence bag. By now, I'd gotten through to the operator, and they were sending out help.

"Let's see your tire," he muttered, marching past me. I trotted to keep up, sliding once in the snow.

"What's the matter with you? You don't have to stay. Roadside assistance is coming out with a new tire."

Frank didn't slow down. "What's the matter with me? How about the fact that someone apparently wishes you enough harm that they slashed your tire in front of a burning house? Why would they do that? And even more importantly, you didn't notice someone running right up to you with a knife. That could have been your throat!"

"Yeah, but I wasn't in the van. I had to go run to the end of the street to get the address," I said, feeling defensive.

"Face it. You have no idea when it happened because you didn't see him."

"Or her," I added.

He wasn't listening. He'd found the tire and squatted down next to it. Curse words flew out of his mouth as he lifted a flap of rubber. A scowl crossed his face.

"What?" I asked.

"Why didn't you tell me sooner?"

"Tell you?" I was flabbergasted. "There were a few things going on when you got here, you know."

His face relaxed. "Oh, never mind. This was the favor you were asking for."

"Favor?" I had no idea what he was talking about.

"Earlier. The text message."

I buried my face in my jacket to hide my laugh. Oh, yeah. I'd forgotten about that. "Actually, I was asking for your help in trapping a few squirrels."

He was taking pictures of my tire, when his face turned to me in surprise. "Squirrels? You serious?"

"Yeah. Not for me. For Oscar. I guess they got into his attic."

He rolled his eyes. Not answering me, he keyed up his shoulder mic and called in a code.

The mic squawked with a, "Copy that."

He stood up with a wince, holding his back like it hurt. "So, it's squirrels, huh? Fine. I'll do it."

"You will? Thank you so much."

"But..." He held a finger up. "You're going with me."

"I ... am?"

"Yep. If I have to crawl around in some old guy's attic with a herd of rabid squirrels, I'm going to need a wingman."

I laughed, the jacket muffling it. "You got it."

"Go get in your van and warm up. I need to take a few more pictures."

I did as he advised, holding my hands over the heater vent. Old Bella might spout exhaust, but she sure could crank the heat. My hands felt like two claws, but after a few minutes, they slowly uncurled.

It was getting dark, but I could see Frank moving about, pausing here and there. He talked with the firemen and wandered around back of the yard. I was waiting for him to come back when the repair truck turned down the road.

I got out and waved the repair guy down. It took less than fifteen minutes for him to put a new tire on my car and a hefty bill in my palm, and then I was back in the driver's seat, rubbing my temples, trying to chase away the headache I felt moving in. A tap on my window nearly gave me a heart attack. It was Frank, again.

I rolled down the window.

"Footprints." As always, he was straight to the point. He rubbed his hands and blew into them.

"Oh, really? Behind the house?"

He nodded, his jaw clenching. "Came around the back and

disappeared into the brush between the properties. I can see where they came to the road. Probably where your van was."

"Why would someone want to slash my tire? It would seem like he'd rather I get away."

"It was a warning, Georgie. Telling you to butt out."

"I don't really see how I've butt in yet." I grinned.

"Always the jokester. You know, there are times you should be taking things more seriously."

"Yeah. I know, Frank. I got it. Anyway, I should get going. Sorry, again for worrying you."

He took a step back and I shifted the van into gear. I waved out the window and carefully drove through the frozen land homeward.

I was tempted to drive around and veg out, which was once my usual way of hiding from my emotions. It had worked for me for the last year. I'd just drive until I ended up someplace I'd never been. Then, I'd be ready to go back home.

But since seeing the counselor, I'd been trying new ways to cope. It had been sixteen months now since Derek died. Since the moment my life changed forever.

I'd blamed myself. I'd blamed him. I'd told myself that I was okay to live as just half a person for the rest of my life.

The first thing my grief counselor had asked me was about the things that had drawn me to love Derek. I'd answered with tears and a smile.

But it was when she asked what I thought he'd say to me now, that I'd lost my words. The lump had been too big in my throat, and just remembering it now was making it grow again.

I knew what he would say. He'd tell me that he loved me and that he loved life. And that me hiding from life was the very thing that would hurt him the most. So for him, for his love for me, I was trying to face life again.

Writing lists was my new coping tool. Instead of car drives to run away, I went home and grabbed a pen and paper and wrote down the things that mattered to me.

Sometimes they were big things. Like Cecelia. A warm place to live. My health.

And sometimes they were small. A red autumn leaf I'd seen. The smell of fresh-baked cookies. New socks.

I drove to my apartment building and parked in the one snowy spot left half a block down. I grabbed the basket— might as well not let it go to waste. The sidewalks had been salted and the slush made little splashes as I walked.

My apartment glowed warmly, and I mentally patted myself

on the back for finally remembering to leave a light on. I dished up some food, stuck it in the microwave, and then got into some pajamas.

Then I found my notebook. Opened to where I'd left off on my list. I wrote the first thing that came to mind that was important to me.

Frank.

I smiled as I saw his name there.

The microwave dinged. I shut the notebook and tucked it back onto my bookshelf. I got my food and flipped the TV on to one of my potato chip shows—those types of shows you can watch for entertainment, and not remember anything about it the next day. I needed to relax and recharge.

The memorial was tomorrow.

CHAPTER 18

I woke the next morning to the sound of the cell phone ringing. I reached over to the side table and, after slapping around a few times, found the phone.

"Hello?" I croaked.

"GiGi! You ready, love?" Cecelia's cheerful voice rang through the receiver. I held it from my hear and winced. *Ready? Ready for what?*

"Um," I said, hedging for time.

"The memorial. It starts in twenty minutes."

I sat straight up in bed. Those words had the power to electrocute me into motion. "Almost," I lied.

"Well, get on down here."

"You're here?"

"Yes. And I don't have the mind to be climbing four flights this early in the morning. So hurry up!"

"Give me five minutes," I said, and hung up before she could answer. I jumped out of bed and caught my reflection in the door mirror. Maybe fifteen.

I ran into the bathroom and grabbed my dry shampoo. Turning upside down, I sprayed my roots like crazy, wiggling around as I danced out of my pajamas. I grabbed my brush and started brushing while racing back to my closet.

What do I have? What do I have? The only black thing I owned was a dress. I swallowed as I saw it—remembering the last funeral I'd attended—and pushed it down the rod and out of sight.

I opted for a pair of dark blue slacks and a sweater. I slipped into them and ran back to the bathroom to examine my hair.

Not too bad. I brushed it back and found my eyeliner and mascara. Quickly, I finished my eyebrows, brushed my teeth, then turned to look for my boots. On the way, I glanced at the clock.

Eight minutes. I'm a flipping rock star.

After grabbing my jacket and purse, I ran out the door with a backwards longing glance at my coffee pot. But there just wasn't any time.

I jogged down the stairs, my hands sliding on the varnished bannister and my feet thudding on the old wood treads. Outside, the cold air was like a smack in the face. I buried my nose in my jacket and looked for Cecelia's car.

There she was, idling double parked, waiting for me. I hurried over and climbed inside.

"Hi." I slammed the door shut.

"Hi, yourself." She smiled at me. Her eyes gave me a quick appraisal. "You look wonderful!"

"Thanks," I said. "Took less than ten minutes to look this good."

I heard a chuckle from the back seat and saw Frank there.

"Good morning to you, too," I said, still snuggling down in my jacket. My body was mad at having been thrown out of a warm bed and into the freezing cold air.

Cecelia put the car into gear. Slowly, we drove down the road, which was surprisingly busy. It only took a minute to realize most of the cars were headed in the same direction as us, St. John's Cathedral.

The church parking was tight, with the added issue of not

being able to see the painted stall lines buried under the snow. Several attendants must have shoveled this morning, because there were clear, salted pathways up to the front doors. Cecelia found a spot and then, after adjusting her hat and buttoning her wool coat, got out. Frank and I followed.

Most of the attendees were the local high school students, by the looks of them. I didn't see any overt displays of grief, but you never knew what people were really thinking.

Cecelia slipped, and I offered her my arm. We walked up the concrete steps, with her hanging heavily to the metal railing.

Right inside the doorway was a large poster board with Patrick Armstrong's picture. His eyes. Good heavens, his eyes. It brought me back to the last time I'd seen them, as his life drained away.

"Is there a bathroom?" I asked, suddenly nauseous.

"You okay, GiGi?"

I shook my head, my hand now over my mouth.

One of the ushers stepped forward. "It's right over there."

I hurried in that direction, feeling horrible to run away before I made it into the sanctuary. But I'd feel worse if I vomited right there and then.

Once in the bathroom, I ran over to the sink and got my hands wet. I rubbed the cool water on the back of my neck and on my cheeks. Deep breath, slow breaths, I reminded myself. My counselor had recommended a trick: breathe in through the nose for a slow count of five, hold it for the count of six, and blow it out through my mouth for the count of seven.

With my eyes closed, I practiced the breathing a few times. It seemed to work. I felt steadier.

There was a cough, making my eyes pop open. Someone else was in the bathroom with me. I grabbed a few paper towels to dry off my neck and face, when the stall door opened.

A young woman came out. Her cheeks had the blotchy appearance of a hard cry. She didn't make eye contact with me, and instead walked straight to the sink.

I dabbed at my neck a little more and tossed the towel in the trash. Our eyes caught in the mirror. Her expression tugged on my heart.

"I'm so sorry," I said. I didn't know her or how she was related to Patrick, but I could see she was in pain.

That was it. It just took those few words to undo the control she'd tried so hard to hang on to.

"Oh, honey," I said. She turned and clung to me like I was her mother. I patted her back. I knew no words could fix this.

She clung to me as her body shuddered with sobs. I

continued to pat and murmur that she could let it out. After a minute, she pulled away and dabbed under her eyes.

"I'm so sorry," she whispered.

"No, it's fine. It's what we're here for."

"I didn't think I'd fall apart like this. I just cared about him so much."

My stomach gave a squeeze as a reminder to my earlier nausea. I remembered all the rumors flying around when he first came to our school, and then the quarterback... How close had she been to him? I was scared to ask and just rubbed her shoulder instead.

The young woman wiped under her eyes and examined her makeup. "He was a life-saver to me. After I graduated last year, he helped me through a really hard time when my parents divorced. He's the one who encouraged me to go to college. He's the one who believed in me. He believed in all of us. Even Ben, the quarterback. Don't believe the lies that he was taking money from the students to pass them. He always tried to give us chances."

She shrugged, her shoulders painfully thin. "I don't know where I would have ended up if he hadn't helped me."

I studied her closely. She didn't seem like she was lying. And it matched all the cards I'd seen in his classroom.

She must have caught the look in my eye. "He didn't do anything inappropriate or anything like that. He was so stodgy and old fashioned, but he was also caring. It's hard to find caring people in this world. You have to believe me."

"I believe you," I said. "This is a really weird question. I don't suppose... in the times you hung out, did he ever talk to you about a special antique he might have had? I think it's missing, and I'm trying to track it down."

She grinned then, just a tiny one, but the first sign that told me she was going to be okay. "It's a secret, but yes."

"I heard it's a secret. But I think someone might have stolen it. Maybe even been the one behind the switched musket." I worded it as gently as possible.

Her eyes widened, darkly fringed with thick lashes. "This is about the pistols?"

Adrenaline flushed through my veins at her words. It was true. I was right. I was right!

"You saw them?" I asked.

She nodded, her gaze darting to the door. It opened then, and a woman in her sixties walked in.

The woman caught sight of us and paused. "Oh. I'm sorry."

"No, it's fine," I reassured her, feeling like the timing was anything but fine.

She nodded as if still not sure, and disappeared into one of the stalls.

The girl's gaze cut between the stall and me. I could feel her anxiety amp up. I didn't want her to run through the doors when I was so close to finding out what I'd been searching for.

"So, my name's Georgie," I said to stall for time.

She smiled again, this time giving me the polite one we do when first meeting a person. "Rebecca."

"Who are you here with?" I asked.

"My mom," she whispered. "Things are better between us now."

"Oh, that's good."

The toilet flushed and the woman came out, still looking quite uncomfortable. She washed her hands quickly with an apologetic grin and left before her hands were completely dry.

As soon as the door was shut, I asked, "Can you tell me anything about the pistols?"

Rebecca shook her head. I was starting to feel disappointed until she said, "But I know that they belonged to George Washington."

"How did he find them?" I whispered, rubbing my arms. I had goose bumps.

She shrugged. "That's all I know."

I patted her shoulder. "Thank you for sharing this with me. I think this is going to help bring justice for Patrick."

She smiled again. "I'd do anything for him."

"Go live your life, and live it well," I said. "That's the best way to pay him back."

She said she would, and disappeared through the door. I turned back toward the mirror, so excited I was shaking. I was close. Very close.

Organ music vibrated through the walls. "Okay, pull it together," I told myself. "Go check on Christopher."

With a deep breath, I exited the bathroom. The foyer was empty, with everyone already behind the closed doors. I started for them when movement caught the corner of my eye.

I turned to look.

A man in black jeans and a black jacket, the hood pulled up to cover his face, was hurrying up the stairs to the second floor.

CHAPTER 19

*I*mmediately, I was suspicious, followed by confusion about what I should do. Did I follow him? But then what would I say if I caught up with the person? Hey, I just wanted to see who you were, despite the fact you might be going up here to be alone and grieve, and I'm stomping all over that privacy like an elephant on grapes?

But something about him bothered me. I didn't think I could let it go without at least checking.

An elephant it is. I tiptoed up the stairs after him. I could hear a deep whisper as I climbed, making me slow down.

"You said you had something good to show me. Where are you?"

My breath caught in my throat. I stood frozen two steps from the top.

"You want to meet at the firearms' shop?" There was a long pause and then, "You got it, boss. I'll check it out."

His voice sounded farther away. I chanced a peek around the corner just in time to see the man disappear out a second-story exterior door that led to outside stairs.

The organ grew louder, the music reverberating upstairs through the speakers. I clambered back down the stairs and opened the front door.

Just snow and slush. No man in black running anywhere.

My heart was hammering as I stood there, not sure of what to do. Go get Frank? But what could he do? I played the conversation over in my mind, trying to decide if it was truly incriminating.

The music played louder. An usher tapped my shoulder.

"Can you please be seated? We're starting now." His eyebrows slanted downward in a disapproving expression.

I took a deep breath. There was nothing I could do at the moment. Who knew where the man was now. I could feel I was frowning hard, so I did my best to smooth out my face as I nodded in the usher's direction and entered the sanctuary.

The place was packed, with a huge wreath of flowers up at the front. They'd moved Patrick's picture there, too. Towards the back, I saw Kari and her husband. I looked for Cecelia and saw she was sitting in the middle with Frank. I started to go towards them but remembered my promise to check on Christopher.

It was just as I suspected. He was sitting alone in the front row, with the seat next to him empty.

I felt intensely guilty as I sidled up the aisle in front of all the onlookers. I could just feel their stares—you're late!—as the organist finished the song.

Christopher stared straight ahead. I gently touched his shoulder.

"Is this seat taken?" I gestured to the empty space.

He glanced over and shook his head. As I took the seat, his face flashed with gratitude. I patted his shoulder.

"I'm so sorry," I whispered.

"Thank you," he answered back, his eyes lined in red.

The service was sweet. I listened as students stood at the podium and spoke of a teacher's passion for history. Even Christopher walked up to share some of his childhood memories of his brother. Before I came this morning, I didn't think I would have been able to attend another memorial. But somehow, hearing the stories, I was comforted that even though our loved ones were gone, they would never be forgotten. They truly to lived on in our hearts.

The organist began the final song, and we stood to sing Amazing Grace. I looked up at the stained glass window, the sun peeking behind and making it glow. In my mind, I waved to Derek.

After the service closed, people began to line up to express their condolences to Christopher. I waited a moment, but he seemed to be doing okay, so I went to find Cecelia.

"How are you feeling?" she asked. "I was worried."

"I'm better." So much had happened since I'd last seen her. I eyed Frank across the room, trying to signal I needed to talk.

It was as if he knew all the craziness I was feeling. He came over and gave me a hug. If anyone could understand loss, it was him.

"You okay, kid?" he asked.

Inside, I was a hodgepodge of emotions, from Rebecca, to the man in black, to Derek. There was no way to address all of it, so I nodded, feeling grateful for his hug.

We stayed for a while, doing the general small talk. The scent of food filled the air—lasagna and chicken—and the pastor invited us all to the dining hall downstairs.

I looked for Rebecca, but she was buttoned up with her mom and a few friends. She seemed okay, laughing at what one of her friends said. We went downstairs and I finally got my cup of coffee.

Cecelia and Frank waited in the food line while I stood to the side, not wanting to stir up the nausea again.

Dane Evans, the quarterback's dad, glared at me from at the other end of the line. At least, I thought he was glaring. Maybe he gave that look to everyone.

I felt a pat on my arm and saw Kari and Joe.

"Hey, lady. I've been hearing things." Kari's blonde hair was pulled up in a bun. She hung on to Joe's arm, her face creased with an expression of concern.

"I know, it's been a bizarre few days," I admitted.

The two of them looked behind me. I glanced back to see Christopher standing there, waiting.

"Seems like he wants to talk with you, so I'll let you go. Call me!" She made a phone sign against her ear as Joe steered her toward the food line.

I faced Christopher. "How are you? Did you get something to eat?"

"Aw, no." He eyed the food line with a shake of his head.

"Just can't stomach it right now. Hey, I just wanted to say I appreciated you coming today."

"Of course. Again, I'm so sorry." I hesitated a moment. "And I'm so sorry about the fire."

He snorted. "Yeah, the hits just keep coming, don't they? Who knows what was in that house that I'll never get back? I know people usually say that things can be replaced, but some things just can't. Anyway, I'll have to deal with the insurance on that. I think I have a case to prove he had something valuable in the house."

"What kind of proof do you have?"

"This." He clicked on his phone and showed me the screen. On it was a picture of Patrick Armstrong with the pistols in his hand.

I was confused. "If you had that picture all along, why did you need me to come search the house? You said you didn't know what you were looking for."

"I didn't. It wasn't until you showed me the article that I realized the significance of this picture. I honestly had no idea what he was holding." Christopher glanced down at it. "He sent it a few years back. He must have just gotten them and was excited, and I think, drunk."

"Why drunk?" I asked.

"Because I never heard from him unless he was drinking."

I frowned but didn't say anything. That certainly didn't match up with he person described by the students and Rebecca. Then again, that might explain why he was so stubborn about the black walnut tree.

But in my heart, I knew why he was stubborn about the tree. More than anything, that man cared about preserving history.

I wondered what the exact nature of the relationship was between these two brothers. Something just didn't add up.

"So." His eyes narrowed. "The police told me that someone slashed your tire at the house. I'm sorry. Did you see who did it?"

I shook my head. "You heard about that? I wouldn't want to bother you after everything you're going through." I sighed. "No, I didn't see them."

"You're a lucky woman." He clapped my shoulder. "I'm just thankful you weren't hurt."

"Thank you. Me, too." I smiled.

Just then, another guest walked up to us. Apparently, Christopher knew him, because they started talking animatedly. I waved goodbye and walked away, not wanting to intrude.

Eventually, I found Cecelia, and we mingled for a little longer. Finally, we collected Frank and said our goodbyes.

The sun was shining as we walked toward the front door, creating a thousand fire rainbows in the snow. Frank opened the door and held it for us.

As I walked through, I caught a glimpse of Dane again. He was standing near the street, talking with a man in the black jacket, the same one who'd run up the stairs earlier. While I watched, the two of them got into a car and took off.

CHAPTER 20

"Hey." I tugged on Frank's arm. "Did you just see that guy? The one at the memorial all in black?"

He narrowed one eye at me. "With that sharp description, I'm sure I know exactly the man you're talking about. Wearing black at a funeral. Hard to miss."

"Well, he *was* all in black. He looked like a stove pipe." We walked across the parking lot, our feet crunching in the snow. Cecelia was ahead of us, heading to the car like a bee making straight for the hive. I could hear her mutter, "Brrr," from here.

He shook his head. "Can't say anyone of that description is standing out to me. Why, Georgie?"

I bit my lip, trying to put my finger on it. "He seemed odd. Ran upstairs at the beginning of the service. I followed him." I caught the look he gave me and hurried on. "I overheard him saying something about a firearms' shop. And, just now, I saw him talking with Dane Evans, the quarterback's dad. They got in a car together and left."

We reached our car then, with Cecelia huddled inside, heat blasting.

He yanked the door open for me. "I trust your gut. Tell me why he first stood out to you."

I climbed in and he got into the back.

"What stood out to you?" Cecelia asked. "Wasn't that service wonderful?"

I said yes the same moment Frank said, "Meh."

"Franklin James Wagner," Cecelia scolded, "that's not very Christian of you!"

"What?" He shrugged. "It was a funeral. It was long. The food lines were long, and I didn't know the guy." His gaze caught mine. "Now, finish telling me what bugged you about the guy."

"Well, like I said, I thought it was weird for him to run upstairs at the start of the service."

"Who are you talking about?" Cecelia asked.

"Some guy I saw dressed all in black," I answered, that description making me feel about as sharp as a wet noodle. "He had on a black jacket with the hood pulled up. I saw him later talking to Dane Evans."

"Oh, him? I overheard him asking someone where his brother, Dane, was. He just arrived on the bus." Cecelia said, shifting the car into drive. The snow and ice churned under the tires as she eased forward.

"Oh." I suddenly felt foolish. "Then there's that."

Frank leaned back in his seat and stared out the window.

"You going to come bake with me today?" Cecelia asked, completely oblivious at how my bright idea had been destroyed by her common sense statement.

"What are you making?" I asked out of politeness, not feeling it at all.

"Chocolate fudgy marshmallow whips."

Hmmm, maybe she could tempt me. My stomach let out a growl, reminding me it had definitely settled down and I hadn't had anything to eat yet.

"Okay, sounds fun." I sat back against the seat with a smile. "But don't have big expectations for me."

"Sweetheart, if I could bake with you when you were eight and jumping all over the kitchen like a jackrabbit, then I can certainly teach you now. You're going to be an expert by the time I'm done with you."

"Okay. I actually wanted to try this technique I saw on TV, a cinnamon roll with parchment paper."

"Oh, that's easy as pie. We'll try it another time. But today is for my fudgies. I've been looking forward to making them all week."

Her and me both.

"Frank, you helping us?" Cecelia glanced at her grandson in the rearview mirror.

"Hmm, probably not. Looks like I have to track down some traps." His tone held a tinge of grumpiness. I stared out my window and tried not to smile.

"Traps?" Cecelia asked.

"Yeah. Apparently our little Julia Childs up there volunteered me to be the great squirrel hunter for your next-door neighbor."

"Oh, Oscar. Poor man." Cecelia pursed her lips and shook her head. We hit an especially big pile of slush, making it fly. Her hands squeezed the steering wheel tighter. "He's got squirrels now?"

171

"Up in his attic, I guess." Frank's voice was glum.

"I said I'd help you." I chanced a look back.

He raised an eyebrow. "I don't recall that's the way it went down. I think I said you will be helping me, to which you made a pitiful whimpering sound."

Cecelia snorted. "Well, you're getting help and doing a good deed. Proud of you, grandson."

Frank shook his head. "You got me good," he muttered, his lip teasing into an almost smile. I was so close. Maybe I could push him over the edge and get a full-fledged smile from him.

"Sounds like you'll need me there to make sure you don't squirrel around," I said with a wink.

Nope. Didn't work. Instead, he rolled his eyes and stared back out the window.

Cecelia pulled down Baker Street with the promise that she'd drive me home later. She parked and the three of us trudged through the snow up to the B&B.

Inside was warm with the scent of cinnamon.

Cecelia rubbed her hands together and adjusted the thermostat. "Come on, GiGi," she called.

I followed her into the kitchen, where we washed our hands.

Then, as she directed, I got out the flour, cocoa powder, butter, and marshmallows from the freezer.

She handed me her recipe card. "I'm passing on the baton," she said with a grin.

I read the card, written in her lacy handwriting. A chocolatey thumbprint from a long-ago cookie adventure decorated one corner.

AUNT CECELIA'S FUDGY MARSHMALLOWS

1/2 cup butter

1/2 cup brown sugar packed

1/2 cup white sugar

1 egg

1 teaspoon vanilla

1 3/4 cup flour

1/4 cup unsweetened cocoa powder

1 teaspoon baking soda

1/2 teaspoon salt

1 cup chocolate chips

1 1/2 cups frozen miniature marshmallows

2 tablespoons milk

DIRECTIONS:

Preheat oven to 375

Mix the butter and sugar

Add in the egg, milk, and vanilla

Add flour, salt, baking soda, and cocoa

Add chocolate chips

Scoop out a spoonful. Lightly roll into a ball. Indent center and put in 3-4 frozen marshmallows. Mold the dough until it covers the marshmallows. Place on cookie sheet.

Makes approximately a dozen

Bake at 375 for eight minutes

I STARTED TO MAKE THEM, feeling like Cecelia had me under her eagle eye. But whenever I snuck a peek at her, she was drinking her coffee and working on her crossword puzzle.

I did hear her suck in her breath when I pulled out the tablespoon instead of the teaspoon to scoop out the baking soda, and shot her a glance. But, just like the other times, she was scribbling away.

It took me longer than it probably should have, but soon I had a dozen cookies on the sheet ready for the oven. I had to admit, I was a bit proud of myself. I stuck them in the oven, and washed everything up.

Eight minutes later on the dot, I pulled out the pan and carefully transferred the gooey treasures to the wire cooling racks.

They looked flipping awesome. I thought even the top chef on the TV show would have given me a high-five on these beauties.

"You did good," Cecelia said as she brought her mug to the sink. She broke a cookie in half and took a bite, "mmming" with exaggerated enjoyment. "Delicious! And now I must figure out some menu planning for next week's guests." She went over to her pantry with her list to work.

I smiled and got a couple of cookies myself and set them on a plate to finish cooling. I took them over to the table and grabbed a pen and junk mail envelope. Something about baking seemed to soothe my mind, allowing me to consider the clues one more time. Turning the envelope over, I started a list.

Where did the fatal musket come from?

The knife that slashed my tire?

Who was the second name on the business card?

Note found at base of tree.

The magazine article about the pistols in the envelope.

Was there anything weird about football dad and the guy in the black jacket?

I bit into the cookie, warm and sweet, and pondered my list. This wasn't working. With a sigh, I grabbed another piece of junk mail from the pile and started a new list.

SUSPECTS AND MOTIVES

Football dad: kid lost scholarship

Brother: insurance and inheritance. Awfully interested in the missing relic.

Gym teacher: blackmail.

Terry: stupid lawsuit over tree.

I had hated to write his name on the list, but I had to. I couldn't entirely rule him out. After another moment, I scribbled one more name after his.

Emily Brooks

The back door banged open. "It's starting to really dump outside again. Grandma, I'll take Georgie home," Frank said, stomping his feet to get rid of the snow.

I glanced at the clock. It was already two.

"Okay, just let me grab my things." I found my purse and jacket, and kissed Cecelia on the cheek. "Thank you for teaching me some of your tricks."

"You're so welcome. I love having a baking partner. Next week, we'll try almond biscotti. Or sugar cookies!" Her pink cheeks rounded as she smiled. "That'll be fun!"

Frank made impatient sounds as the two of us giggled. I laced up my boots, and together we headed outside.

The wind shot right through my thin coat like it was made of tissue. Snow swirled around and hit my face. "Holy cow!"

"Yeah, it's cold out here." Frank's nose and cheeks were red from his earlier trip outside.

"You find some traps?"

He nodded. "Grandma had a couple in her shed. I'll bring them over to Oscar tomorrow."

We climbed into the car, and I shivered as Frank started it and turned up the heat. Cold air blasted me.

"Brr!" I yelled.

"Give it a second. She warms up real fast."

He backed out of the driveway, tires spinning once, and then we were on the road. The daylight had that quiet, blurry look from the clouds and snow.

We drove in silence for a few minutes. Finally, he cleared his throat and asked, "You starting to get warm?" He adjusted the heat's vent to blow my way.

"Better, thank you."

"So, how are you doing being back? Getting settled?"

"I've been back over a year, Frank," I said teasingly.

"I know. I know. I just remember how it took me a long while to get used to things after I got back." He gave an ironic grin. "I'm still not sure I am."

It *was* strange to be back home. He was right about that. I'd left Gainesville with a head full of dreams, pretty sure I knew who I was.

Came back with no idea what I wanted and all my dreams shattered.

"I remember feeling kind of disillusioned," he said, stating exactly how I felt.

I nodded. "Life is weird. But oddly comforting in its weirdness."

"Comforting, huh?" He flipped the blinker and merged into traffic. The snow hit the windshield with little ticks instead of fat splats, indicating the temperature was dropping.

"Yeah. There's lots of unexpected surprises tucked in the corners."

"Most people don't like surprises," he noted.

I laughed, agreeing. "Well, I don't really either. But then you make a friend where you didn't expect one, or get money, discover a new restaurant, see a deer... It's looking forward to those things that keeps me going. You never know what's around the corner."

The corner of his eye crinkled, and I could tell he was thinking. "I think I'm getting old," he said, to which I snorted since I was the exact same age. "No, I'm serious. Like when I think back to us growing up, it feels like the good old days. Only I didn't know what I had back then."

"How do you feel about your time in the army?" I asked.

He sighed. "Wow. Is that a loaded question, or what? I loved it. Hated it. Was bored a lot of the time. But I knew what I was doing, and why I was there. I felt like I was making a difference."

"Do you still keep in contact with the people you met there?"

"Some. I'll always have their back." He shot a sideways glance at me. "How about you? Still talking with the people from your fancy law firm?"

"Not really. Things changed. People moved on. Life goes on." I stared out the window.

He nodded. It was getting a little too heavy, so I changed the subject. "Do you remember Terry from school? I don't know if you had any classes with him."

"Algebra two. Horrible class. Never used the math. Ever."

I laughed again. "Me either. Should have taken the cooking class like my grandma suggested. But about Terry, from what you remember, do you think he could have done it?"

He sighed, his nostrils flaring. His blue eyes caught mine for a second, and I could see the answer there. But what he said was, "That's not my job to judge. My job's to bring in the suspects and let the detectives and prosecutors make their cases. Because, in the end, it's still innocent until proven guilty."

I nodded and chewed on my thumbnail.

"But I'd like to see him go free," he added. "I guess time will tell."

"What do you think about Jared Inglewood?"

"The gym teacher? He's up there on the suspect list. Posted

bail as soon as he got to jail. But I heard the prosecutor is going to the grand jury to have him arrested on embezzling the school program funds."

"That's a big deal. That kind of thing makes a man desperate."

"Yeah. Desperate enough to kill a woman who just witnessed him breaking and entering. You lucked out on that one." He shook his head.

"Won't happen again," I promised.

"Good. Can't have me always saving the day," he said. I started to protest and he winked. "I'm kidding. You did okay on your own." He slowed to a stop outside my apartment. "All right, here we are."

"Thanks for the ride," I said, opening the door.

"Get a good night's sleep," he yelled as I climbed out. "Because we're going squirrel hunting tomorrow!"

Squirrel hunting or not, I couldn't help the smile on my face as I shut the car door.

CHAPTER 21

I was still smiling when I unlocked my apartment door. Wow. The feeling kind of caught me off guard. How long had it been since I'd felt truly felt happy? Was it him making me feel this way? This was crazy. Maybe it was a sugar high. I did eat about six of them.

I thought about Derek. Like a snake swallowing a mouse, the happiness disappeared, replaced with a feeling of disloyalty.

I set the cookies on the counter with a sigh. Memories came flooding in at Derek's name, as if called like a genie from a lamp.

Things like splashing in the Atlantic Ocean the first time either of us had seen it, driving through Pittsburgh traffic with him stressing out that we were late, taking that trip to Maine and eating fresh lobster.

Then a memory of Frank came. It was during the winter of our senior year, a winter similar to this one, cold and snowy.

We'd both volunteered for an organization that helped the homeless as part of our senior project. I'd never really understood the harsh reality of homelessness until I saw someone shivering while using a ratty cardboard box as a shelter from the falling snow.

We'd given out socks, blankets, and information about the nearest shelter. Every other week, we spent a day at the shelter, handing out food. I remember the expression on Frank's face when he knelt down to tie an older woman's boots. They'd been men's boots and were enormous on her feet. She'd been telling him about the family she'd once had, speaking with a lisp through her missing teeth. Her clothing was stained, but she still had a cheery expression on her ruddy cheeks. She patted his head like he was a pup, and he'd had a smile on his face when he looked up. But I'd seen how he'd blinked hard while tying those boots.

That guy was always trying to help someone.

The phone rang, breaking my reverie. I dug for it in my purse and checked the screen. I didn't recognize the number.

"Hello?" I answered.

"Hi, Georgie. It's Christopher." His voice held a bit of worry. "I got your number from your aunt. I hope I'm not disturbing you."

Cecelia? That was odd. "Oh, hello. How are you? I bet you're exhausted from the memorial this morning."

He chuckled. "I'm totally beat, but I think I found something very interesting. I wanted to call you right away."

My ears perked up with interest. "What is it?"

"It was in the box of stuff the school sent over. A note I found in one of the books."

I grimaced, mentally kicking myself that I hadn't checked the books.

"Don't laugh, but I just get this feeling like you might know what it's referring to."

"What does it say?"

"It says, 'If you're reading this, I need you to take a history lesson, lest history repeat itself. Remember my character. I stand for it.'" He hesitated. "What do you think it means?"

"It's where he hid the pistols," I said, chills running down my spine.

"Seriously?" His voice trilled with excitement. "Where?"

I stopped for a second, his eagerness reminding me. "Did you talk with anyone from the Museum of American History?"

My comment was met with silence, and then a small laugh. "Yeah, they contacted me after Patrick died. They were pretty worried the deal was off, but I told them I knew where the pistols were. Talked to them just yesterday. They're pretty interested in what I have."

"I can imagine. That's a great place to give the pistols."

"Give?" He snickered.

I'd admit, the snicker gave me a pause. But, after all, the historian part of me figured I'd rather have the pistols kept safe for the public. I was excited to be a part of the process of getting them to a museum.

"Anyway, I think I know where he stashed them," I said.

"Tell me," he said.

"Well, he mentions history repeating itself. Like it does every year for the reenactment. And then he says, remember my character. That's Colonel Berkshire. His grave is in a mausoleum in the center of the Gainesville cemetery."

"You think they're there?"

"I'm almost positive." I couldn't keep the enthusiasm out of my voice.

"Well, all right then! Let's go! Want to meet me there?"

"I'd loved to."

"I have the number of the guy at the museum. I can see if he's still interested."

"Oh, he'll be interested, all right," I assured him. "But you should wait until we see if it's really them."

"All right, when can you come?"

I thought about how far the cemetery was. "Let me grab a quick bite to eat. And the roads are slick. Let's say in an hour."

We hung up and I made myself a sandwich and carried it into the bedroom, taking a big bite as I went. Chewing, I pulled on a second sweater to layer up. I didn't want to be cold this time.

Something was bothering me about all of this. Something just wasn't adding up. I glanced at the clock. Okay, I had a few minutes.

Hurrying to my laptop, I lifted the screen and searched up the museum. I took another bite as the search engine brought up several choices. The same red banner welcomed and tried to entice me to sign up so I could hear about the up-and-coming exhibit.

To the left was a list of the curator names. I scrolled through them, finding Charles Vanderstill listed with the rest.

I chewed thoughtfully.

This time, I did a regular search on his name. After a moment, the search engine spat out some acceptable results. Name: Charles Vanderstill. Occupation: Curator at the New York City Museum of United States history. Age: 72.

My heart ramped up. I wanted to warn Christopher, but his phone went straight to voice mail. I crammed the rest of my sandwich into my mouth and grabbed my jacket and purse.

About twenty minutes later, I pulled into at the cemetery parking lot. My brain was running full speed ahead, trying to make sense of all of this, as I walked towards the entrance.

Christopher was already standing there, jiggling on his toes and looking cold.

So was Charles Vanderstill.

"Georgie." Christopher waved at me with a big smile on his face, before blowing on his hands.

Standing as tall as my five-foot-two would let me, I walked over to the duo.

"Hey, what are you doing here?" I asked Charles, trying to give an easygoing smile. How could I warn Christopher?

Christopher answered for him. "I told you, he called me a couple days ago. He said he'd been discussing the pistols with Patrick, and actually had been in the area to get them the day he died."

I shook my head, ever so subtly. Immediately, I tried to pass it off like I was trying to scratch my neck.

But it was too late. I could tell by the way Charles narrowed eyes that he'd noticed.

"Georgie. What's the matter? You that surprised to see me?" Charles' voice was hearty.

"I...I'm just shocked," I stammered. Licking my lips, I tried to smile again.

"It's fate!" Christopher was acting like a kid with an Easter egg basket. "I called him after you, and he said he happened to be back in town. It seemed like a no-brainer to have him meet us out here."

It was Christopher's words that made me realize I'd only assumed Charles had gone back home. I cringed at how I'd believed he'd really been on his way to a lecture. He'd probably been running around a hotel room, just waiting for his moment to find those pistols.

I watched Charles edge closer to Christopher and felt sick.

I tried to act subtle and think fast. "It sure is cold! My nose is running." I rummaged through my purse for my phone.

"I wouldn't do that if I were you," Charles said, his voice carrying a sharp edge, making me stop.

Something about Charles' eyes finally seemed to alert Christopher. "What's going on?" He looked between the two of us, two lines forming between his brows.

"Why, Christopher. You were just getting ready to show us the pistols you said you found." Charles took another step closer, his face red from the wind. He grabbed Christopher's arm, in a friendly but firm way.

Christopher looked down at Charles' hand clapped to his arm. He turned to me. "Maybe you should go, Georgie. I'll catch you lat—" His voice squawked and his face went white.

Charles now had his hand shoved into Christopher's side.

"How did you know the pistols weren't in the Armstrong house?" I asked Charles.

"I didn't know that," Charles answered.

"Then why did you set the house on fire?"

"Fire?" He laughed and his good-looking face broke into a sneer. "Little lady, I didn't set anything on fire." He drove the nose of the pistol harder into Christopher's side. "At least, not yet."

CHAPTER 22

Charles' lips curled into a creepy smile, the kind you see on those plastic Joker masks. "Like I said, Georgie. It's a surprise, but I'm glad I could bump into you again. Christopher asked me to meet him at this park. But I had no idea that you had been invited to the party as well."

"I searched for Charles Vanderstill. He does work for the museum, but he's about thirty years older than you." I watched him warily.

"I'm impressed. No one's looked him up before. His identity was the easiest to assume. I just needed a few of his business cards, which was quite easy to accomplish."

"Who are you really?" I asked, stalling for time. Someone had to be coming by. The cemetery was never this empty.

He laughed, sounding colder than the wind knifing through my jacket. "Who I am is not important. Let's say I'm in the procurement business. People hire me to get what they want. Rich people. Someone heard Patrick had contacted the museum looking to sell his pistols. That little bit of news made it to me. I was happy to intercept them on their way there. What made you search me up anyway? Or Charles, I should say."

"That business card in Patrick's drawer. When I called, you said you'd never met Patrick, but that it had been Christopher who had contacted you. Christopher had never visited the school to possibly deposit the business card into the desk drawer. Besides, Christopher also said that it was you who contacted him after his brother died. But, supposedly, you'd already gone home. Remember? I called you, and you were teaching a 'seminar.'"

His smile dropped to fifty percent and his eyes narrowed. I felt like I was caught in the gaze of a cobra.

But I was the mongoose. "When you went for coffee that morning, I remember being a little surprised when you said you couldn't find a coffee stand. But that's when you were switching the muskets, right? You were the one that grilled the teenagers at the armory table that day. You brought the musket and told one of them that Armstrong insisted Terry use it. You told the other

191

one that the musket was Terry's. Did you steal that, too?"

"Steal? I don't think so. First you accuse me of setting his house on fire, and now stealing a musket. You aren't very good at this."

"You weren't going go meet Patrick to purchase the pistols, but to steal them. But he must have outsmarted you somehow for you to be standing here right now, empty handed."

"He showed me the box in the trunk of his car, and we planned to do the trade after his little reenactment thingy. Killing him was my mistake. I thought I was tidying up my loose ends. But when I went back out to his car during all the commotion, I was quite disappointed to see that the box was empty. It seems he'd actually spoken with the real Charles Vanderstill earlier, so when I made contact, he was thrown off by my voice. When he asked me about it, I told him that I was Mr. Draken, Charles' personal assistant. Fortunately, the museum was closed, and I assumed we'd have this all cleared up before he had a chance to call again. I thought he believed me. It turns out he was an even better actor than I was."

The wind blew, causing the little American flags marking the graves to flutter. I shivered, but this time not because I was cold.

Charles smiled, fake and unpleasant. "Now let's get moving. Where did you say they were again?" These last words were whispered into Christopher's ear.

I tried one more time to discreetly pull out my cell phone to call for the police.

"I told you I wouldn't do that." Charles rammed the pistol even harder into Christopher's ribs. "Just lead me to what I want, and I'll be on my way."

Christopher swallowed hard, and I saw his Adam's apple bob. He was pale now and sweating. "She knows. She's the one who told me to come here." He pointed to me. "Tell him, Georgie!" he insisted.

"I think they're in the mausoleum at the center of the cemetery." My voice sounded higher than usual. I breathed slowly, trying to steady myself. I wasn't sure what was going to happen, but if I wanted a chance, I had to stay calm.

Charles nodded. "Let's go check it out."

"Can't you let us go? Check it out for yourself," Christopher pleaded. "We won't say anything. We don't even know your real name."

"That doesn't really matter. I can be whoever I want to be. You'll never see me again." His eyes mocked me and he motioned with his head to lead. Christopher followed behind with Charles next to him.

The trees here grew scattered between the graves. The graves were old, mostly from the Civil War era, but as we got deeper into the cemetery, we started seeing the truly old ones. Crumbling stone markers, worn down by time. Most of them could barely be read.

At the cemetery's center was a bronze statue of Colonel Berkshire. He stood with his musket atop a stone mausoleum. The building had a gate around it to protect it from vandals.

The gate had a newer chain and lock on it. Charles motioned to the gate. "Unlock it."

I shook my head, my mouth suddenly dry. "I don't have the key."

The man growled and quickly swung the pistol around and shot the cheap chain, separating it. The cast iron gate swung inward.

"Go get it." He waved to Christopher and then to the building. "You have five minutes before I shoot her and come in after you."

I had chosen the moment that he went to shoot the chain to ease my cell from my purse and down to my side. As the shot rang out, I dialed the preset 911 and jammed the phone into my pocket. I didn't know if the call went through, or if emergency services could really track my call, or if that was just for the movies. Maybe they'd just sum it up as a prank. But it was my only chance.

Christopher walked to the building, which was held shut with a rusty latch. It looked like there might have been a lock on it at one point, but it was gone now.

"Get over here," Charles said, pushing me closer to the fence opening. He glanced around at the surrounding area, checking that it was empty. The wind caused the tree branches to scrape together. I shivered at the sound. My movement caused a sharp glance from him. His finger slid down to the trigger.

"Are you just going to take the pistols and go?" I hurriedly asked, trying to distract him.

"Something like that." He stared into the mausoleum opening.

"You know, you could even lock us in there. No one would find us for a long while."

He looked like he was considering it. Then he nudged the broken chain with the nose of his pistol. "Can't keep you secure."

I swallowed hard. To me, his words meant he was definitely planning to shoot us.

I tried again, gesturing to the neighborhood I knew was on the other side of the glade of trees. "One gunshot, these neighbors will ignore. But two, three? They'll be calling the cops. A few of them will probably even come running. You won't escape."

"You let me worry about that."

"You'll have what you want. Just leave us here. We won't tell anyone. You can even use your jacket to tie the bars shut."

"You know what else a jacket is good for?" He tapped my head with the nose of his pistol, and the hair on the back of my neck stood up. "It does a fairly decent job as a silencer at close range. So shut your mouth."

I had to work doubly hard to control my breathing. Christopher still hadn't emerged. Maybe he was in there hatching his own plan. Maybe he even had his phone. He could be calling the police right this minute.

Charles must have noticed an expression of hope flash across my face. He glanced at the opening again. "What do you think is going on in there, princess? You think he's trying to get those old saddle pistols to work? Or, do you think he might be using his phone to call for help?"

I watched him warily.

He laughed. "Those pistols won't work without a ton of restoration. He tries to use them on me and he's liable to blow his own head off. Save me the trouble. And as for his phone, well, he left that in the car. He was talking to me when I pulled up. The idiot waved at me and hung up, leaving his phone on the dashboard. Apparently, he's not as attached to it as some people."

Hope drained out of me, leaving my legs feeling like gelatin. I'd been so sure that was the reason Christopher was taking so long.

Don't give up. You can do this. I glanced around for anything that could be used as a weapon. There wasn't much. Just a few scattered flags poking out of slots by the headstones, and a handful of dead flowers in a vase by the gate's entrance.

"Christopher!" Charles called. "You have thirty seconds before I shoot her and come in after you."

"They have cameras," I said. My heart was hammering so hard it felt like my whole body was pulsing. "Right at the entrance. They'll be able to identify you."

"They might see me. But exactly who will they see? Just the person I am today. I have many, many identities."

The scraping sound coming from the dark doorway told us little about what was going on inside. As Christopher materialized from the shadows, he carried a bundle of cloth, possibly concealing the antique pistols.

Charles' hand seemed to grip his pistol tighter. I just needed more time. "Unwrap it, Christopher," I said. "Make sure it's the real deal."

"Good idea," Charles said. "Show me what we've got here."

Christopher's hands trembled as he began to slowly unwrap the package. All three of us held our breath. Charles leaned forward, just a hair, his eyes glowing with anticipation.

I glanced down at the vase. It was such a small thing. Would it work? I'd make it work. As Christopher unwrapped the final flap, showing the beautiful antique pistols, Charles took a breath in. I crouched and grabbed the vase.

Charles looked over, catching my movement. His pistol came up, but not before I smashed the vase right into his face.

Christopher lunged forward and ripped the loose chain away from the gate. "Move, Georgie!" he yelled. He whipped the chain across the back of Charles' head. Charles stumbled forward, stunned, and fell to the ground. I jumped in and snatched the pistol from his hands.

My hands were shaking as I held it. I watched Christopher twist Charles' arms behind his back and pin him down.

I yanked my phone out of my pocket. It was still connected. "Hello?" I yelled.

"911, we have police already on the way."

"You tracked us?" I could feel tears of gratitude sting my eyes.

"We certainly did. They're en route." The operator asked a few more questions and for a description our exact location. I answered, feeling like I was in a dream.

The entire time, I kept a close eye on Charles. The nose of the pistol was pointed down, but I wasn't afraid to bring it up if I had to.

Christopher impressed me, showing amazing stamina, pinning the man down for the time it took for the police to show up. When they arrived, he fell back, exhausted, his eyes wide. He kept repeating over and over, "I can't believe that just happened."

I'd have replied, but I saw Frank hustling across the cemetery toward me. That poor man. I'd put him through more stress in these last few days than anyone deserved.

This time, it was me pulling Frank into a tight hug as the other officers handcuffed Charles and hauled him away. The police took the antique pistols in as evidence, making Christopher blanche, but they assured him that he would get them back soon.

"Can you believe that just happened?" Christopher asked me.

"Yeah. Life is weird," I said, but he probably didn't hear me. My face was still buried against Frank's chest.

And I didn't care anymore what anyone had to say. I just wanted to close my eyes and be held.

CHAPTER 23

I spent the next few hours at the police station giving another interview. It was rewarding to get to be there when they released Terry. He came back and found me at Jefferson's desk—poor Jefferson, that man was probably sick of taking my statements—and gave me a big hug.

"You did it again, champ," he said. "You saved my bacon."

"You know me, always got to stick my nose in where it doesn't belong," I tried to joke.

He gave my arm a light punch, which made Frank's eyebrow lift, and then waved goodbye. I could hear his wife squeal when she saw him from all the way in the front of the precinct. Made my heart happy.

"Look at you grinning like you just won the Nobel Peace Prize," Frank noted. I laughed, but I had to admit, I was really pleased at how it all worked out.

"You ready to go home?" he asked, when Jefferson finally said he was done with me.

I nodded.

"Well, too bad, because we still have squirrel hunting left on the calendar."

"What? Oh, come on. You said tomorrow."

"Hey, I've got you out of the house now. It's only six. Besides, it serves you right for practically grave robbing that monument."

"It wasn't grave robbing. Patrick Armstrong hid them there." I contemplated that for about a second. "He must have removed the lock, or maybe there wasn't one. I remember the lock on the gate was new. Anyway, I think it was Charles that Emily saw go up to his door that day. Patrick probably freaked out when Charles introduced himself, having spoken to the real Charles in New York City."

"And he tried to cover by saying he was the assistant, Draken."

"Yeah, which explains Patrick's note. Call Charles, don't trust Draken."

We got into his car, and I resigned myself to some squirrel hunting. "I wish I knew who Charles was really."

"We're running his fingerprints now, but we think he's one of the big-wigs of a known antique and art theft ring. It's those types the museum was worried about. People find out that an ancient relic's been found and everyone tries to jump on it. Then they sell it on the black market to the highest bidder."

We pulled into the Baker Street B&B, and I got hugged and scolded for the next twenty minutes by Cecelia.

When she finally let me get a word in edgewise, I apologized. Honestly, it was the only thing I could do. "I promise I won't hit any more bad guys in the face with a vase," I said.

The words weren't even fully out of my mouth and she was swatting my arm. "You keep that sassy tone out of your voice, Missy! I'm serious. You could have been killed."

I didn't want her to ramp up again, so I quickly agreed. "I won't do it again. I promise."

She eyed me suspiciously before giving me another hug. "I don't know what I would do without my GiGi!"

I hugged her back and marveled at how even her clothing and hair seemed to carry the scent of cinnamon and vanilla.

Frank leaned against the countertop and watched us. "Glad

you lectured her, Grandma. I've been trying. You'd think she would have learned after her tire got slashed."

"Hey. That wasn't my fault. Patrick's house was on fire. I actually saved the day on that one."

Cecelia shook her head. "Why on earth would that bad man set Patrick's house on fire? Poor Christopher."

I turned to face Frank. "That's right. Charles didn't seem to know anything about the fire."

Frank whistled. "We got some footage from one of those doorbell cameras. Neighbor had one installed across the street. It looks like Jared Inglewood returned to finish the job."

"The job?" Cecelia asked.

"He'd been searching for some evidence that Patrick supposedly had on him. The prosecutor had just requested a search order from the judge. Somehow Jared got word and torched the place."

"But why slash my tire?" I asked, feeling confused.

"Who knows. Anger? Revenge? It *was* your fault that he was caught."

Cecelia shook her head at me. Finally, after another kiss on my cheek and swat on my arm, I was free to follow Frank over to Oscar's place. Honestly, I didn't know which was worse, being left to Cecelia's scolding or being forced to hunt squirrels.

Oscar was his usual cheerful self when he answered the door. He stood in his worn slippers, Peanut in his arms, and took in Frank, his eyebrows raising above his glasses. "Well, looky here. Paul Bunyan and his newfangled dealy-bobs are probably going to come crashing through my ceiling."

Frank's eyes narrowed at the old man's tone. I made the introductions, trying to keep the smile off my face. Frank might have met his match in the grouch department.

Shuffling slowly, Oscar led us to the trap door to the attic. "And don't blame me if them squirrels bite you," he added as Frank pulled down the ladder. Frigid air swirled out. "I've seen their eyes! They're crazy!"

"I'll be careful," Frank reassured him, before staring up into the black opening. Pink insulation poked out from the edges of the crawlspace. He took a deep breath and adjusted his headlamp to direct the beam ahead of him. Rustling came from somewhere inside, and we both flinched.

"You ready?" he growled at me.

I nodded, feeling like this was hardly better than the cemetery situation.

He didn't see me nod, but he must have taken my silence as agreement, because he started up the ladder. The ladder shuddered under his weight. I thought I'd better wait at the bottom until he got up there. Heck, he might not even need m—

"Get up here, Tanner. I'm not doing this alone."

Quickly, I scrambled up the ladder after him. He had heaved himself to the side and was looking around the attic by the time I poked my head through the opening.

"You need help climbing up?" he asked.

"I can do it," I said, and hauled myself up onto the floor.

His face was stern as he studied the space, the beam from the headlamp leading the way. "Here, I brought you this," he said, picking another headlamp out from his shirt pocket.

I slid it over my head and switched it on. Our beams looked like they were sword fighting as they crossed paths.

The attic was filled with boxes, more than I dreamed of. I knew Cecelia said Oscar had been here nine or ten years, but there was a lifetime represented by the cardboard stacks before me. Boxes labeled photos, blankets, grandma's linens, silver tea set, magazines. I choked up a bit when I read one that said boy's baby clothes.

His wife must have marked all of these, who knew how long ago. And here they sat... forgotten.

The scurrying sounds started again, this time at the other end of the attic. My eyes widened.

"Follow me," Frank said. "Watch your step. Stay on the plywood or the floor joists."

He didn't have to tell me twice. The last thing I wanted was to fall halfway through the ceiling, and dangle there, stuck, while Oscar yelled at me from below.

The dust was thick, with tufts of insulation peeking out under the makeshift floor. We crawled along. There wasn't quite enough space to stand up.

As if Frank knew what I was thinking, he cautioned, "Watch your head." With that, he glanced up, allowing the beam to flash along a few exposed nails sticking out of the rafters.

"Got it," I muttered, crawling nearly at his heels. He crawled to the vent, pushing the trap before him. Moonlight shined through the vent. It was obvious that the screen had been pushed in. Under the beam of his headlamp, he unbent the metal and re-hooked the screen on the nail. Then he glanced around, grumbling until he spotted a two-by-four stub. He used the stub to pound the nail down, securing the screen.

"All right. Now there's just this." He dragged the trap closer. "You having fun yet?" His teeth gleamed white in the bit of light from the vent.

"So much," I said. I could taste the dust in my mouth.

He chuckled. The sound just about made me fall over. I stared at him, and he held his hand up to ward off the headlamp's beam. "Hey, look somewhere else, would ya?"

"Oh, sorry. It's just been ages since I heard you laugh." I thought about that for a minute. "Maybe the first time ever."

"Aw, come on. I laugh." He opened the trap's door and set it carefully. He reached into his pocket and grabbed out one of Cecelia's cookies and crumbled it up inside.

"Mmmhmm," I said, noncommittally.

"What?" He sat back on his heels and flipped his light up so he could face me. "You don't think I laugh? Like ever?"

"You were the serious one of us. Of course it might have been because I was such a brat," I said.

He smiled again. "That you were. But I had a lot of fun. I have a ton of good memories."

"Really?"

Rubbing the back of his neck, he looked a little sheepish. "Yeah. They're what kept me going at times."

"Stop. You're kidding me."

"Seriously. Hey, I can prove it." He hesitated, and then shook his head. "Never mind."

"What? You can't just leave it at that!"

He gazed at me, his blue eyes drawing me in. "You're going to think it's weird. It is weird." He glanced up at the ceiling. "What have I started?"

"What is it? Just tell me."

Nervously, his tongue wet his bottom lip, and then he seemed to decide. With a resigned sigh, he pulled his wallet out of his back pocket. "Yeah, um, so this is going to freak you out. But this got me through some real tough times in Afghanistan." He flipped open the billfold and poked around. After a minute, he pulled out a dog-eared photograph. He stared at it a moment, with a ghost of a smile on his lips, before passing it over.

I gasped when I saw it. It'd been taken during the summer after our senior year. Cecelia and Grandma had made us do yard work all day, and afterwards, we'd gone to the watering hole to take advantage of the last rays of sunlight. I could see Kari, blurry in the background. Whoever was taking the picture must have called Frank and me because we were both staring at the camera.

"You're smiling," I said, touching his face in the photo. I looked at him now.

His face was serious, his eyes studying me to catch my reaction. When he met my eyes, the corner of his lip lifted, just barely. "Yeah, well, it made me smile every time I saw it. To think of you doing those cannon balls off the bank. Splashing me until I dunked you." He softly chuckled. "It was nice to remember."

I couldn't believe it. He'd had my picture all these years... and it had helped him?

He glanced at me again, his eyebrows rising slightly.

There was a question there.

I swallowed as my stomach fluttered with butterflies. I knew it was about time for me to answer that question.

I couldn't keep the smile from my face. It warmed my heart that I'd been able to make him smile when he needed it the most, and I realized that I really, really wanted to keep doing that for a little while more.

The End

Thank you for reading Cookies and Scream. Keep an eye out for book three in the Bakers Street Cozy Mysteries, Crème Brûlée or Slay, and book four, Drizzle of Death

If you're hungry for more cozy mysteries, be sure to check out my Oceanside Hotel Cozy Mystery series or my Angel Lake Cozy Mystery series. Thank you again!

Printed in Poland
by Amazon Fulfillment
Poland Sp. z o.o., Wrocław